PENGUIN BOOKS

TIME STOPS AT SHAMLI

Ruskin Bond was born in Kasauli in 1934. He has written several novels, short stories and books for children in the course of a long writing career. *The Room on the Roof* (also published by Penguin), written when the author was only 17, won the John Llewellyn Rhys Memorial Prize in 1957.

Ruskin Bond lives in Mussoorie.

TIME STOPS AT SHAMLI

AND OTHER STORIES

RUSKIN BOND

To
Rony
with love and best wishes
krishna thasu
& dadu
11. 7. 08

PENGUIN BOOKS

PENGUIN BOOKS
Published by the Penguin Group
Penguin Books India Pvt. Ltd, 11 Community Centre, Panchsheel Park, New Delhi
110 017, India
Penguin Group (USA) Inc., 375 Hudson Street, New York, New York 10014, USA
Penguin Group (Canada), 90 Eglinton Avenue East, Suite 700, Toronto, Ontario,
M4P 2Y3, Canada (a division of Pearson Penguin Canada Inc.)
Penguin Books Ltd, 80 Strand, London WC2R 0RL, England
Penguin Ireland, 25 St Stephen's Green, Dublin 2, Ireland (a division of Penguin
Books Ltd)
Penguin Group (Australia), 250 Camberwell Road, Camberwell, Victoria 3124,
Australia (a division of Pearson Australia Group Pty Ltd)
Penguin Group (NZ), 67 Apollo Drive, Rosedale, North Shore 0632, New Zealand
(a division of Pearson New Zealand Ltd)
Penguin Group (South Africa) (Pty) Ltd, 24 Sturdee Avenue, Rosebank, Johannesburg
2196, South Africa

Penguin Books Ltd, Registered Offices: 80 Strand, London WC2R 0RL, England

First published by Penguin Books India 1989

20 19 18 17 16

Some of these stories first appeared in *Short Story International*, the *Asia Magazine*,
Blackwoods, the *Illustrated Weekly of India*, the *Sunday Standard* and various
other newspapers and magazines.

Typeset in ITC Garamond by SAMHITA, Hyderabad
Printed at Anubha Printers, Noida

*Dedicated
to the memory of
my Grandfather,
William Dudley Clerke*

Contents

Introduction

Some say the real India is to be found in its villages; others would like to think that India is best represented by its big cities and industrial centres. For me, India has always been an atmosphere, an emotional more than a geographical entity; but if I have to transpose this rather nebulous concept into something more concrete, then I would say that India is really to be found in its small towns.

Small-town India—that's *my* India. The India of Shamli and Shahganj, Panipat and Pipalkoti, Alwar and Ambala and Alleppey, Kalka and Kasauli and Kolar Goldfields, and thousands of others along the rivers, along the coasts, straddling the mountains or breaking up the monotony of scrub and desert. Taken together, they set the cities at naught. They are the heart of India, an untapped source of vast human potential, largely ignored except when elections come round.

I suppose I'm prejudiced, being a small-town boy myself. My bio-data simply reads: Born in Kasauli, small boy in Jamnagar, bigger boy in Dehra Dun, schoolboy in Simla, sundry adventures in Agra, Ambala and Rishikesh, and now holed up in Mussoorie! *Dihli dur ast....* Delhi is a far cry. And Bombay, where have *you* been all my life? Have I missed something very precious? Have I, in choosing the dusty lanes of Roorkee or Shahjahanpur, missed out on the sights of Calcutta and Madras, or lost my last chance to lean against the leaning tower of Pisa or savour the aromas of the Venetian canals? If I have, so be it. Our own aromas are sufficiently interesting. I will continue to write of the residents of Gali Ram Rai and other *mohallas*, and leave it to more restless souls to sing the praises of five-star cuisine and the fascinating world of airports after dark.

Small towns don't change in the way that cities change. It is still possible to find the old landmarks and sometimes the old people. There is a timelessness about small-town and cantonment India that I have tried to capture in a story like 'Time Stops at Shamli'. It begins like 'The Night Train at Deoli' in my earlier collection, but this time I step off the train, explore the place, discover a boarding-house inhabited by a number of

9

lonely individuals living in a time capsule like my own, meet an old love, and discover a few things about myself before continuing my journey. We are all ships that pass in the night.

'The Funeral' is the most recent story in this collection. It describes an incident that is as fresh in my mind today as it was almost fifty years ago. When it comes to loving and living and dying, there is no such thing as being modern and fashionable. Some things will never change. For it isn't time that's passing by, my friend; it is you and I.

Growing up isn't painful all the time. In 'The Room of Many Colours' I describe the magical childhood I experienced before my father's death. The anguish I have often felt at the rapid disappearance of our forest and animal wealth is expressed in 'Tiger, Tiger, Burning Bright' in which I identify with the tiger, a loner in a rapidly changing environment. The empathy I have for birds and animals even extends to the world of the crow. In 'A Crow for All Seasons' I *became* a crow—and great fun it was too.

Occasionally I have indulged myself in the ghost story, of which there are two or three examples in this collection (as there were in the earlier collection). Ghosts are intangibles and can mean different things to different people, and one of these days I must devote a separate book to them. An early practitioner of the form, who had some influence on me, was Lafcadio Hearn (1850–1904), one of the most neglected writers in this genre. As a freelancer in America he was so badly paid that he frequently slept in the streets; he went to Japan and finally found recognition there for his superb stories of the supernatural. In an essay on ghost stories he wrote: 'The ghostly always represents some shadow of truth. The ghost story has always happened in our dreams and reminds us of forgotten experiences, imaginative and emotional . . . .' Hence its appeal.

I have nearly always enjoyed myself in my writing. And if some of that enjoyment has been conveyed to the reader, then I have achieved what I set out to do, and no prizes are solicited.

Mussoorie   RUSKIN BOND
1 April 1989

The Funeral

'I don't think he should go,' said Aunt M.

'He's too small,' concurred Aunt B. 'He'll get upset and probably throw a tantrum. And you know Padre Lal doesn't like having children at funerals.'

The boy said nothing. He sat in the darkest corner of the darkened room, his face revealing nothing of what he thought and felt. His father's coffin lay in the next room, the lid fastened forever over the tired, wistful countenance of the man who had meant so much to the boy. Nobody else had mattered—neither uncles nor aunts nor fond grandparents; least of all the mother who was hundreds of miles away with another husband. He hadn't seen her since he was four—that was just over five years ago—and he did not remember her very well.

The house was full of people—friends, relatives, neighbours. Some had tried to fuss over him but had been discouraged by his silence, the absence of tears. The more understanding of them had kept their distance.

Scattered words of condolence passed back and forth like dragonflies on the wind. 'Such a tragedy!'. . . .'Only forty'. . . .'No one realized how serious it was'. . . .'Devoted to the child'. . . .

It seemed to the boy that everyone who mattered in the hill-station was present. And for the first time they had the run of the house; for his father had not been a sociable man. Books, music, flowers and his stamp collection had been his main preoccupations, apart from the boy.

A small hearse, drawn by a hill pony, was led in at the gate, and several able-bodied men lifted the coffin and manoeuvred it into the carriage. The crowd drifted away. The cemetery was about a mile down the road, and those who did not have cars would have to walk the distance.

The boy stared through a window at the small procession passing through the gate. He'd been forgotten for the moment—left in care of the servants, who were the only ones to stay behind. Outside, it was misty. The mist had crept up the valley and settled like a damp towel on the face of the mountain. Everyone was wet, although it hadn't rained.

The boy waited until everyone had gone, and then he left the room and went out on the verandah. The gardener, who had been sitting in a bed of nasturtiums, looked up and asked the boy if he needed anything; but the boy shook his head and retreated indoors. The gardener, looking aggrieved because of the damage done to the flower-beds by the mourners, shambled off to his quarters. The *sahib's* death meant that he would be out of job very soon. The house would pass into other hands, the boy would go to an orphanage. There weren't many people who kept gardeners these days. In the kitchen, the cook was busy preparing the only big meal ever served in the house. All those relatives, and the Padre too, would come back famished, ready for a sombre but nevertheless substantial meal. He too would be out of job soon; but cooks were always in demand.

The boy slipped out of the house by a back-door and made his way into the lane through a gap in a thicket of dog-roses. When he reached the main road, he could see the mourners wending their way round the hill to the cemetery. He followed at a distance.

It was the same road he had often taken with his father during their evening walks. The boy knew the name of almost every plant and wildflower that grew on the hillside. These, and various birds and insects, had been described and pointed out to him by his father.

Looking northwards, he could see the higher ranges of the Himalayas and the eternal snows. The graves in the cemetery were so laid out that if their incumbents did happen to rise one day, the first thing they would see would be the glint of the sun on those snow-covered peaks. Possibly the site had been chosen for the view. But to the boy it did not seem as if anyone would be able to thrust aside those massive tombstones and rise from their graves to enjoy the view. Their rest seemed as eternal as the snows. It would take an earthquake to burst those stones asunder and thrust the coffins up from the earth. The boy wondered why people hadn't made it easier for the dead to rise. They were so securely entombed that it appeared as though no

12

one really wanted them to get out.

'God has need of your father. . . .' In those words a well-meaning missionary had tried to console him.

And had God, in the same way, laid claim to the thousands of men, women and children who had been put to rest here in these neat and serried rows? What could he have wanted them for? Of what use are we to God when we are dead, wondered the boy.

The cemetery gate stood open, but the boy leant against the old stone wall and stared down at the mourners as they shuffled about with the unease of a batsman about to face a very fast bowler. Only this bowler was invisible and would come up stealthily and from behind.

Padre Lal's voice droned on through the funeral service, and then the coffin was lowered—down, deep down—the boy was surprised at how far down it seemed to go! Was that other, better world down in the depths of the earth? How could anyone, even a Samson, push his way back to the surface again? Superman did it in comics, but his father was a gentle soul who wouldn't fight too hard against the earth and the grass and the roots of tiny trees. Or perhaps he'd grow into a tree and escape that way! 'If ever I'm put away like this,' thought the boy, 'I'll get into the root of a plant and then I'll become a flower and then maybe a bird will come and carry my seed away. . . . I'll get out somehow!'

A few more words from the Padre, and then some of those present threw handfuls of earth over the coffin before moving away.

Slowly, in twos and threes, the mourners departed. The mist swallowed them up. They did not see the boy behind the wall. They were getting hungry.

He stood there until they had all gone, then he noticed that the gardeners or caretakers were filling in the grave. He did not know whether to go forward or not. He was a little afraid. And it was too late now. The grave was almost covered.

He turned and walked away from the cemetery. The road stretched ahead of him, empty, swathed in mist. He was alone. What had his father said to him once? 'The strongest man in the world is he who stands alone.'

Well, he was alone, but at the moment he did not feel very

strong.

·For a moment he thought his father was beside him, that they were together on one of their long walks. Instinctively he put out his hand, expecting his father's warm, comforting touch. But there was nothing there, nothing, no one. . . .

He clenched his fists and pushed them deep down into his pockets. He lowered his head so that no one would see his tears. There were people in the mist, but he did not want to go near them, for they had put his father away.

'He'll find a way out,' the boy said fiercely to himself. 'He'll get out somehow!'

The Room of Many Colours

Last week I wrote a story, and all the time I was writing it I thought it was a good story; but when it was finished and I had read it through, I found that there was something missing, that it didn't ring true. So I tore it up. I wrote a poem, about an old man sleeping in the sun, and this was true, but it was finished quickly, and once again I was left with the problem of what to write next. And I remembered my father, who taught me to write; and I thought, why not write about my father, and about the trees we planted, and about the people I knew while growing up and about what happened on the way to growing up. . . .

And so, like Alice, I must begin at the beginning, and in the beginning there was this red insect, just like a velvet button, which I found on the front lawn of the bungalow. The grass was still wet with overnight rain.

I placed the insect on the palm of my hand and took it into the house to show my father.

'Look, Dad,' I said, 'I haven't seen an insect like this before. Where has it come from?'

'Where did you find it?' he asked.

'On the grass.'

'It must have come down from the sky,' he said. 'It must have come down with the rain.'

Later he told me how the insect really happened but I preferred his first explanation. It was more fun to have it dropping from the sky.

I was seven at the time, and my father was thirty-seven, but, right from the beginning, he made me feel that I was old enough to talk to him about everything—insects, people, trees, steam-engines, King George, comics, crocodiles, the Mahatma, the Viceroy, America, Mozambique and Timbuctoo. We took long walks together, explored old ruins, chased butterflies and

15

waved to passing trains.

My mother had gone away when I was four, and I had very
dim memories of her. Most other children had their mothers
with them, and I found it a bit strange that mine couldn't stay.
Whenever I asked my father why she'd gone, he'd say, 'You'll
understand when you grow up.' And if I asked him *where* she'd
gone, he'd look troubled and say, 'I really don't know.' This was
the only question of mine to which he didn't have an answer.

But I was quite happy living alone with my father; I had never
known any other kind of life.

We were sitting on an old wall, looking out to sea at a couple
of Arab dhows and a tramp steamer, when my father said,
'Would you like to go to sea one day?'

'Where does the sea go?' I asked.

'It goes everywhere.'

'Does it go to the end of the world?'

'It goes right round the world. It's a round world.'

'It can't be.'

'It is. But it's so big, you can't see the roundness. When a fly
sits on a water-melon, it can't see right round the melon, can it?
The melon must seem quite flat to the fly. Well, in comparison
to the world, we're much, much smaller than the tiniest of
insects.'

'Have you been around the world?' I asked.

'No, only as far as England. That's where your grandfather was
born.'

'And my grandmother?'

'She came to India from Norway when she was quite small.
Norway is a cold land, with mountains and snow, and the sea
cutting deep into the land. I was there as a boy. It's very
beautiful, and the people are good and work hard.'

'I'd like to go there.'

'You will, one day. When you are older, I'll take you to
Norway.'

'Is it better than England?'

'It's quite different.'

'Is it better than India?'

'It's quite different.'

'Is India like England?'

'No, it's different.'

'Well, what does "different" mean?'

'It means things are not the same. It means people are different. It means the weather is different. It means trees and birds and insects are different.'

'Are English crocodiles different from Indian crocodiles?'

'They don't have crocodiles in England.'

'Oh, then it must be different.'

'It would be a dull world if it was the same everywhere,' said my father.

He never lost patience with my endless questioning. If he wanted a rest, he would take out his pipe and spend a long time lighting it. If this took very long I'd find something else to do. But sometimes I'd wait patiently until the pipe was drawing, and then return to the attack.

'Will we always be in India?' I asked.

'No, we'll have to go away one day. You see, it's hard to explain, but it isn't really our country.'

'Ayah says it belongs to the King of England, and the jewels in his crown were taken from India, and that when the Indians get their jewels back the King will lose India! But first they have to get the crown from the King, but this is very difficult, she says, because the crown is always on his head. He even sleeps wearing his crown!'

Ayah was my nanny. She loved me deeply, and was always filling my head with strange and wonderful stories.

My father did not comment on ayah's views. All he said was, 'We'll have to go away some day.'

'How long have we been here?' I asked.

'Two hundred years.'

'No, I mean *us.*'

'Well, you were born in India, so that's seven years for you.'

'Then can't I stay here?'

'Do you want to?'

'I want to go across the sea. But can we take *ayah* with us?'

'I don't know, son. Let's walk along the beach.'

*

We lived in an old palace beside a lake. The palace looked like

17

a ruin from the outside, but the rooms were cool and comfortable. We lived in one wing, and my father organized a small school in another wing. His pupils were the children of the Raja and the Raja's relatives. My father had started life in India as a tea-planter; but he had been trained as a teacher and the idea of starting a school in a small state facing the Arabian Sea had appealed to him. The pay wasn't much, but we had a palace to live in, the latest 1938-model Hillman to drive about in, and a number of servants. In those days, of course, everyone had servants (although the servants did not have any!). Ayah was our own; but the cook, the bearer, the gardener, and the *bhisti* were all provided by the state.

Sometimes, I sat in the schoolroom with the other children (who were all much bigger than me), sometimes I remained in the house with ayah sometimes I followed the gardener, Dukhi, about the spacious garden.

Dukhi means 'sad', and, though I never could discover if the gardener had anything to feel sad about, the name certainly suited him. He had grown to resemble the drooping weeds that he was always digging up with a tiny spade. I seldom saw him standing up. He always sat on the ground with his knees well up to his chin, and attacked the weeds from this position. He could spend all day on his haunches, moving about the garden simply by shuffling his feet along the grass.

I tried to imitate his posture, sitting down on my heels and putting my knees into my armpits; but could never hold the position for more than five minutes.

Time had no meaning in a large garden, and Dukhi never hurried. Life, for him, was not a matter of one year succeeding another, but of five seasons—winter, spring, hot weather, monsoon and autumn—arriving and departing. His seedbeds had always to be in readiness for the coming season, and he did not look any further than the next monsoon. It was impossible to tell his age. He may have been thirty-six or eighty-six. He was either very young for his years or very old for them.

Dukhi loved bright colours, especially reds and yellows. He liked strongly scented flowers, like jasmine and honeysuckle. He couldn't understand my father's preference for the more delicately perfumed petunias and sweetpeas. But I shared Dukhi's fondness for the common, bright orange marigold, which is offered in temples and is used to make garlands and nosegays. When the garden was bare of all colour, the marigold would still be there, gay and flashy, challenging the sun.

Dukhi was very fond of making nosegays, and I liked to watch him at work. A sunflower formed the centre-piece. It was surrounded by roses, marigolds and oleander, fringed with green leaves, and bound together with silver thread. The perfume was over-powering. The nosegays were presented to me or my father on special occasions, that is, on a birthday or to guests of my father's who were considered important.

One day I found Dukhi making a nosegay, and said, 'No one is coming today, Dukhi. It isn't even a birthday.'

'It is a birthday, *chota sahib*,' he said. 'Little *sahib*' was the title he had given me. It wasn't much of a title compared to Raja *sahib*, *Diwan sahib* or *Burra sahib* but it was nice to have a title at the age of seven.

'Oh,' I said. 'And is there a party, too?'

'No party.'

'What's the use of a birthday without a party? What's the use of a birthday without presents?'

'This person doesn't like presents—just flowers.'

'Who is it?' I asked, full of curiosity.

'If you want to find out, you can take these flowers to her. She lives right at the top of that far side of the palace. There are twenty-two steps to climb. Remember that, *chota sahib* you take twenty-three steps, you will go over the edge and into the lake!'

I started climbing the stairs.

It was a spiral staircase of wrought iron, and it went round and round and up and up, and it made me quite dizzy and tired.

At the top I found myself on a small balcony, which looked out over the lake and another palace, at the crowded city and the distant harbour. I heard a voice, a rather high, musical voice, saying (in English) 'Are you a ghost?' I turned to see who had spoken but found the balcony empty. The voice had come from a dark room.

I turned to the stairway, ready to flee, but the voice said, 'Oh, don't go, there's nothing to be frightened of!'

And so I stood still, peering cautiously into the darkness of the room.

'First, tell me—are you a ghost?'

'I'm a boy,' I said.

'And I'm a girl. We can be friends. I can't come out there, so you had better come in. Come along, I'm not a ghost either—not yet, anyway!'

As there was nothing very frightening about the voice, I stepped into the room. It was dark inside, and, coming in from the glare, it took me some time to make out the tiny, elderly lady seated on a cushioned, gilt chair. She wore a red sari, lots of coloured bangles on her wrists, and golden ear-rings. Her hair was streaked with white, but her skin was still quite smooth and unlined, and she had large and very beautiful eyes.

'You must be Master Bond!' she said. 'Do you know who I am?'

'You're a lady with a birthday,' I said, 'but that's all I know. Dukhi didn't tell me any more.'

'If you promise to keep it a secret, I'll tell you who I am. You see, everyone thinks I'm mad. Do you think so too?'

'I don't know.'

'Well, you must tell me if you think so,' she said with a chuckle. Her laugh was the sort of sound made by the gecko, the little wall-lizard, coming from deep down in the throat. 'I have a feeling you are a truthful boy. Do you find it very difficult to tell the truth?'

'Sometimes.'

'Sometimes. Of course, there are times when I tell lies—lots of little lies—because they're such fun! But would you call me a liar? I wouldn't, if I were you, but *would* you?'

'Are you a liar?'

'I'm asking you! If I were to tell you that I was a queen—that I *am* a queen—would you believe me?'

I thought deeply about this, and then said, 'I'll try to believe you.'

'Oh, but you *must* believe me. I'm a real queen, I'm a Rani! Look I've got diamonds to prove it!' And she held out her hands, and there was a ring on each finger, the stones glowing and glittering in the dim light. 'Diamonds, rubies, pearls and emeralds! Only a queen can have these!' She was most anxious that I should believe her.

'You must be a queen,' I said.

'Right!' she snapped. 'In that case, would you mind calling me

"Your Highness"?'

'Your Highness,' I said.

She smiled. It was a slow, beautiful smile. All her face lit up.

'I could love you,' she said. 'But better still, I'll give you something to eat. Do you like chocolates?'

'Yes, Your Highness.'

'Well,' she said, taking a box from the table beside her; 'these have come all the way from England. Take two. Only two, mind, otherwise the box will finish before Thursday, and I don't want that to happen because I won't get any more till Saturday. That's when Captain MacWhirr's ship gets in, the S. S. LUCY loaded with boxes and boxes of chocolates!'

'All for you?' I asked in considerable awe.

'Yes, of course. They have to last at least three months. I get them from England. I get only the best chocolates. I like them with pink, crunchy fillings, don't you?'

'Oh, yes!' I exclaimed, full of envy.

'Never mind,' she said. 'I may give you one, now and then— if you're *very* nice to me! Here you are, help yourself. . . .' She pushed the chocolate box towards me.

I took a silver-wrapped chocolate, and then just as I was thinking of taking a second, she quickly took the box away.

'No more!' she said. 'They have to last till Saturday.'

'But I took only *one*,' I said with some indignation.

'Did you?' She gave me a sharp look, decided I was telling the truth, and said graciously, 'Well, in that case you can have another.'

Watching the Rani carefully, in case she snatched the box away again, I selected a second chocolate, this one with a green wrapper. I don't remember what kind of a day it was outside, but I remember the bright green of the chocolate wrapper.

I thought it would be rude to eat the chocolates in front of a queen, so I put them in my pocket and said, 'I'd better go now. Ayah will be looking for me.'

'And when will you be coming to see me again?'

'I don't know,' I said.

'Your Highness.'

'Your Highness.'

'There's something I want you to do for me,' she said, placing one finger on my shoulder and giving me a conspiratorial look.

'Will you do it?'

'What is it Your Highness?'

'What is it? Why do you ask? A real prince never asks where or why or whatever, he simply does what the princess asks of him. When I was princess—before I became a queen, that is—I asked a prince to swim across the lake and fetch me a lily growing on the other bank.'

'And did he get it for you?'

'He drowned half way across. Let *that* be a lesson to you. Never agree to do something without knowing what it is.'

'But I thought you said....'

'Never mind what I *said*. It's what I *say* that matters!'

'Oh, all right,' I said, fidgeting to be gone. 'What is it you want me to do?'

'Nothing.' Her tiny rosebud lips pouted and she stared sullenly at a picture on the wall. Now that my eyes had grown used to the dim light in the room, I noticed that the walls were hung with portraits of stout Rajas and Ranis: turbaned and bedecked in fine clothes. There were also portraits of Queen Victoria and King George V of England. And, in the centre of all this distinguished company, a large picture of mickey mouse.

'I'll do it if it isn't too dangerous.' I said.

'Then listen.' She took my hand and drew me towards her— what a tiny hand she had!—and whispered, 'I want a *red* rose. From the palace garden. But be careful! Don't let Dukhi the gardener catch you. He'll know it's for me. He knows I love roses. And he hates me! I'll tell you why, one day. But if he catches you, he'll do something terrible.'

'To me?'

'No, to himself. That's much worse, isn't it? He'll tie himself into knots, or lie naked on a bed of thorns, or go on a long fast with nothing to eat but fruit, sweets and chicken! So you will be careful, won't you?'

'Oh, but he doesn't hate you,' I cried in protest, remembering the flowers he'd sent for her, and looking around, I found that I'd been sitting on them. 'Look, he sent these flowers for your birthday!'

'Well, if he sent them for my birthday, you can take them back,' she snapped. 'But if he sent them for *me* ....' and she suddenly softened and looked coy, 'then I might keep them.

Thank you, my dear, it was a very sweet thought.' And she leant forward as though to kiss me.

'It's late, I must go!' I said in alarm, and turning on my heels, ran out of the room and down the spiral staircase.

*

Father hadn't started lunch or rather tiffin, as we called it then. He usually waited for me, if I was late. I don't suppose he enjoyed eating alone.

For tiffin we usually had rice, a mutton curry (*koftas* or meat balls, with plenty of gravy, was my favourite curry), fried *dal* and a hot lime or mango pickle. For supper we had English food—a soup, roast pork and fried potatoes, a rich gravy made by my father, and a custard or caramel pudding. My father enjoyed cooking, but it was only in the morning that he found time for it. Breakfast was his own creation. He cooked eggs in a variety of interesting ways, and favoured some Italian recipes which he had collected during a trip to Europe, long before I was born.

In deference to the feelings of our Hindu friends, we did not eat beef; but, apart from mutton and chicken, there was a plentiful supply of other meats—partridge, venison, lobster, and even porcupine!

'And where have you been?' asked my father, helping himself to the rice as soon as he saw me come in.

'To the top of the old palace,' I said.

'Did you meet anyone there?'

'Yes, I met a tiny lady who told me she was a Rani. She gave me chocolates.'

'As a rule, she doesn't like visitors.'

'Oh, she didn't mind me. But is she really a queen?'

'Well, she's the daughter of a Maharaja. That makes her a princess. She never married. There's a story that she fell in love with a commoner, one of the palace servants, and wanted to marry him, but of course they wouldn't allow that. She became very melancholic, and started living all by herself in the old palace. They give her everything she needs, but she doesn't go out or have visitors. Everyone says she's mad.'

'How do they know?' I asked.

'Because she's different from other people, I suppose.'

'Is that being mad?'

'No. Not really, I suppose madness is not *seeing* things as others see them.'

'Is that very bad?'

'No,' said father, who for once was finding it very difficult to explain something to me. 'But people who are like that—people whose minds are so different that they don't think, step by step, as we do, whose thoughts jump all over the place—such people are very difficult to live with....'

'Step by step,' I repeated. 'Step by step....'

'You aren't eating,' said my father. 'Hurry up, and you can come with me to school today.'

I always looked forward to attending my father's classes. He did not take me to the schoolroom very often, because he wanted school to be a treat, to begin with; then, later, the routine wouldn't be so unwelcome.

Sitting there with older children, understanding only half of what they were learning, I felt important and part grown-up. And of course I did learn to read and write, although I first learnt to read upside-down, by means of standing in front of the others' desks and peering across at their books. Later, when I went to school, I had some difficulty in learning to read the right way up; and even today I sometimes read upside-down, for the sake of variety. I don't mean that I read standing on my head; simply that I hold the book upside-down.

I had at my command a number of rhymes and jingles, the most interesting of these being 'Solomon Grundy'.

> Solomon Grundy,
> Born on a Monday,
> Christened on Tuesday,
> Married on Wednesday,
> Took ill on Thursday,
> Worse on Friday,
> Died on Saturday,
> Buried on Sunday:
> This is the end of
> Solomon Grundy.

Was that all that life amounted to, in the end? And were we all Solomon Grundies? These were questions that bothered me, at times.

Another puzzling rhyme was the one that went:

> Hark, hark,
> The dogs do bark,
> The beggars are coming to town;
> Some in rags,
> Some in bags,
> And some in velvet gowns.

This rhyme puzzled me for a long time. There were beggars aplenty in the bazaar, and sometimes they came to the house, and some of them did wear rags and bags (and some nothing at all) and the dogs did bark at them, but the beggar in the velvet gown never came our way.

'Who's this beggar in a velvet gown?' I asked my father.

'Not a beggar at all,' he said.

'Then why call him one?'

And I went to Ayah and asked her the same question, 'Who is the beggar in the velvet gown?'

'Jesus Christ,' said Ayah.

Ayah was a fervent Christian and made me say my prayers at night, even when I was very sleepy. She had, I think, Arab and Negro blood in addition to the blood of Koli fishing community to which her mother had belonged. Her father, a sailor on an Arab dhow, had been a convert to Christianity. Ayah was a large, buxom woman, with heavy hands and feet, and a slow, swaying gait that had all the grace and majesty of a royal elephant. Elephants for all their size, are nimble creatures; and Ayah too, was nimble, sensitive, and gentle with her big hands. Her face was always sweet and childlike.

Although a Christian, she clung to many of the beliefs of her parents, and loved to tell me stories about mischievous spirits and evil spirits, humans who changed into animals, and snakes who had been princes in their former lives.

There was the story of the snake who married a princess. At first the princess did not wish to marry the snake, whom she had met in a forest, but the snake insisted, saying, 'I'll kill you if you won't marry me,' and of course that settled the question. The snake led his bride away and took her to a great treasure. 'I was a prince in my former life,' he explained. 'This treasure is yours.' And then the snake very gallantly disappeared.

'Snakes,' declared Ayah, 'were very lucky omens if seen early in the morning.'

'But what if the snake bites the lucky person?' I asked.

'He will be lucky all the same,' said Ayah with a logic that was all her own.

Snakes! There were a number of them living in the big garden, and my father had advised me to avoid the long grass. But I had seen snakes crossing the road (a lucky omen, according to Ayah) and they were never aggressive.

'A snake won't attack you,' said Father, 'provided you leave it alone. Of course, if you step on one it will probably bite.'

'Are all snakes poisonous?'

'Yes, but only a few are poisonous enough to kill a man. Others use their poison on rats and frogs. A good thing, too, otherwise during the rains the house would be taken over by the frogs.'

One afternoon, while Father was at school, Ayah found a snake in the bath-tub. It wasn't early morning and so the snake couldn't have been a lucky one. Ayah was frightened and ran into the garden calling for help. Dukhi came running. Ayah ordered me to stay outside while they went after the snake.

And it was while I was alone in the garden—an unusual circumstance, since Dukhi was nearly always there—that I remembered the Rani's request. On an impulse, I went to the nearest rose bush and plucked the largest rose, pricking my thumb in the process.

And then, without waiting to see what had happened to the snake (it finally escaped), I started up the steps to the top of the old palace.

When I got to the top, I knocked on the door of the Rani's room. Getting no reply, I walked along the balcony until I reached another doorway. There were wooden panels around the door, with elephants, camels and turbaned warriors carved into it. As the door was open, I walked boldly into the room; then stood still in astonishment. The room was filled with a strange light.

There were windows going right round the room, and each small window-pane was made of different coloured glass. The sun that came through one window flung red and green and purple colours on the figure of the little Rani who stood there with her face pressed to the glass.

She spoke to me without turning from the window. 'This is my favourite room. I have all the colours here. I can see a different world through each pane of glass. Come, join me!' And she beckoned to me, her small hand fluttering like a delicate butterfly.

I went up to the Rani. She was only a little taller than me, and we were able to share the same window-pane.

'See, it's a red world!' she said.

The garden below, the palace and the lake, were all tinted red. I watched the Rani's world for a little while and then touched her on the arm and said, 'I have brought you a rose!'

She started away from me, and her eyes looked frightened. She would not look at the rose.

'Oh, why did you bring it?' she cried, wringing her hands. 'He'll be arrested now!'

'Who'll be arrested?'

'The prince, of course!'

'But *I* took it,' I said. 'No one saw me. Ayah and Dukhi were inside the house, catching a snake.'

'Did they catch it?' she asked, forgetting about the rose.

'I don't know. I didn't wait to see!'

'They should follow the snake, instead of catching it. It may lead them to a treasure. All snakes have treasures to guard.'

This seemed to confirm what Ayah had been telling me, and I resolved that I would follow the next snake that I met.

'Don't you like the rose, then?' I asked.

'Did you steal it?'

'Yes.'

'Good. Flowers should always be stolen. They're more fragrant, then.'

*

Because of a man called Hitler, war had been declared in Europe, and Britain was fighting Germany.

In my comic papers, the Germans were usually shown as blundering idiots; so I didn't see how Britain could possibly lose the war, nor why it should concern India, nor why it should be necessary for my father to join up. But I remember his showing me a newspaper headline which said:

BOMBS FALL ON BUCKINGHAM PALACE—
KING AND QUEEN SAFE

I expect that had something to do with it.

He went to Delhi for an interview with the RAF and I was left in Ayah's charge.

It was a week I remember well, because it was the first time I had been left on my own. That first night I was afraid—afraid of the dark, afraid of the emptiness of the house, afraid of the howling of the jackals outside. The loud ticking of the clock was the only reassuring sound: clocks really made themselves heard in those days! I tried concentrating on the ticking, shutting out other sounds and the menace of the dark, but it wouldn't work. I thought I heard a faint hissing near the bed, and sat up, bathed in perspiration, certain that a snake was in the room. I shouted for Ayah and she came running, switching on all the lights.

'A snake!' I cried. 'There's a snake in the room!'

'Where, *baba*?'

'I don't know where, but I *heard* it.'

Ayah looked under the bed, and behind the chairs and tables, but there was no snake to be found. She persuaded me that I must have heard the breeze whispering in the mosquito-curtains.

But I didn't want to be left alone.

'I'm coming to you,' I said and followed into her small room near the kitchen.

Ayah slept on a low string cot. The mattress was thin, the blanket worn and patched up; but Ayah's warm and solid body made up for the discomfort of the bed. I snuggled up to her and was soon asleep.

I had almost forgotten the Rani in the old palace and was about to pay her a visit when, to my surprise, I found her in the garden.

I had risen early that morning, and had gone running barefoot over the dew-drenched grass. No one was about, but I startled a flock of parrots and the birds rose screeching from a banyan tree and wheeled away to some other corner of the palace grounds. I was just in time to see a mongoose scurrying across the grass with an egg in its mouth. The mongoose must have been raiding the poultry farm at the palace.

I was trying to locate the mongoose's hideout, and was on all fours in a jungle of tall cosmos plants when I heard the rustle of clothes, and turned to find the Rani staring at me.

She didn't ask me what I was doing there, but simply said: 'I don't think he could have gone in there.'

'But I saw him go this way,' I said.

'Nonsense! He doesn't live in this part of the garden. He lives in the roots of the banyan tree.'

'But that's where the snake lives,' I said.

'You mean the snake who was a prince. Well, that's who I'm looking for!'

'A snake who was a prince!' I gaped at the Rani.

She made a gesture of impatience with her butterfly hands, and said, 'Tut, you're only a child, you can't *understand*. The prince lives in the roots of the banyan tree, but he comes out early every morning. Have you seen him?'

'No. But I saw a mongoose.'

The Rani became frightened. 'Oh dear, is there a mongoose in the garden? He might kill the prince!'

'How can a mongoose kill a prince?' I asked.

'You don't understand, Master Bond. Princes, when they die, are born again as snakes.'

'*All* princes?'

'No, only those who die before they can marry.'

'Did your prince die before he could marry you?'

'Yes. And he returned to this garden in the form of a beautiful snake.'

'Well,' I said, 'I hope it wasn't the snake the water-carrier killed last week.'

'He killed a snake!' The Rani looked horrified. She was quivering all over. 'It might have been the prince!'

'It was a brown snake,' I said.

'Oh, then it wasn't him.' She looked very relieved. 'Brown snakes are only ministers and people like that. It has to be a green snake to be a prince.'

'I haven't seen any green snakes here.'

'There's one living in the roots of the banyan tree. You won't kill it, will you?'

'Not if it's really a prince.'

'And you won't let others kill it?'

'I'll tell Ayah.'

'Good. You're on my side. But be careful of the gardener. Keep him away from the banyan tree. He's always killing snakes. I don't trust him at all.'

She came nearer and, leaning forward a little, looked into my eyes.

'Blue eyes—I trust them. But don't trust green eyes. And yellow eyes are evil.'

'I've never seen yellow eyes.'

'That's because you're pure,' she said, and turned away and hurried across the lawn as though she had just remembered a very urgent appointment.

The sun was up, slanting through the branches of the banyan tree, and Ayah's voice could be heard calling me for breakfast.

'Dukhi,' I said, when I found him in the garden later that day. 'Dukhi, don't kill the snake in the banyan tree.'

'A snake in the banyan tree!' he exclaimed, seizing his hoe.

'No, no!' I said. 'I haven't seen it. But the Rani says there's one. She says it was a prince in its former life, and that we shouldn't kill it.'

'Oh,' said Dukhi, smiling to himself. 'The Rani says so. All right, you tell her we won't kill it.'

'Is it true that she was in love with a prince but that he died before she could marry him?'

'Something like that,' said Dukhi. 'It was a long time ago—before I came here.'

'My father says it wasn't a prince, but a commoner. Are you a commoner, Dukhi?'

'A commoner? What's that, *chota sahib*?'

'I'm not sure. Someone very poor, I suppose.'

'Then I must be a commoner,' said Dukhi.

'Were *you* in love with the Rani?' I asked.

Dukhi was so startled that he dropped his hoe and lost his balance; the first time I'd seen him lose his poise while squatting on his haunches.

'Don't say such things, *chota sahib*!'

'Why not?'

'You'll get me into trouble.'

'Then it must be true.'

Dukhi threw up his hands in mock despair and started collecting his implements.

'It's true, it's true!' I cried, dancing round him, and then I ran indoors to Ayah and said, 'Ayah , Dukhi was in love with the Rani!'

Ayah gave a shriek of laughter, then looked very serious and put her finger against my lips.

'Don't say such things,' she said. 'Dukhi is of a very low caste. People won't like it if they hear what you say. And besides, the Rani told you her prince died and turned into a snake. Well, Dukhi hasn't become a snake as yet, has he?'

True, Dukhi didn't look as though he could be anything but a gardener; but I wasn't satisfied with his denials or with Ayah's attempts to still my tongue. Hadn't Dukhi sent the Rani a nosegay?

*

When my father came home, he looked quite pleased with himself.

'What have you brought for me?' was the first question I asked.

He had brought me some new books, a dart-board, and a train set; and in my excitement over examining these gifts, I forgot to ask about the result of his trip.

It was during tiffin that he told me what had happened—and what was going to happen.

'We'll be going away soon,' he said. 'I've joined the Royal Air Force. I'll have to work in Delhi.'

'Oh! Will you be in the war, Dad? Will you fly a plane?'

'No, I'm too old to be flying planes. I'll be forty years in July. The RAF, will be giving me what they call intelligence work— decoding secret messages and things like that and I don't suppose I'll be able to tell you much about it.'

This didn't sound as exciting as flying planes; but it sounded important and rather mysterious.

'Well, I hope it's interesting,' I said. 'Is Delhi a good place to live in?'

'I'm not sure. It will be very hot by the middle of April. And you won't be able to stay with me, Ruskin—not at first, anyway not until I can get married quarters and then, only if your mother returns....Meanwhile, you'll stay with your grandmother in Dehra.' He must have seen the disappointment in my face, because he quickly added: 'Of course I'll come to see you often. Dehra isn't far from Delhi—only a night's train journey.'

But I was dismayed. It wasn't that I didn't want to stay with my grandmother; but I had grown so used to sharing my father's life and even watching him at work, that the thought of being separated from him was unbearable.

'Not as bad as going to boarding-school,' he said. 'And that's the only alternative.'

'Not boarding-school,' I said quickly, 'I'll run away from boarding-school.'

'Well, you won't want to run away from your grandmother. She's very fond of you. And if you come with me to Delhi, you'll be alone all day in a stuffy little hut, while I'm away at work. Sometimes I may have to go on tour—then what happens?'

'I don't mind being on my own.' And this was true: I had already grown accustomed to having my own room and my own trunk and my own bookshelf and I felt as though I was about to lose these things.

'Will Ayah come too?' I asked.

My father looked thoughtful. 'Would you like that?'

'Ayah must come,' I said firmly. 'Otherwise I'll run away.'

'I'll have to ask her,' said my father.

Ayah it turned out, was quite ready to come with us: in fact, she was indignant that Father should have considered leaving her behind. She had brought me up since my mother went away, and she wasn't going to hand over charge to any upstart aunt or governess. She was pleased and excited at the prospect of the move, and this helped to raise my spirits.

'What is Dehra like?' I asked my father.

'It's a green place,' he said. 'It lies in a valley in the foothills of the Himalayas, and it's surrounded by forests. There are lots of trees in Dehra.'

'Does Grandmother's house have trees?'

'Yes. There's a big jackfruit tree in the garden. Your grandmother planted it when I was a boy. And there's an old banyan tree, which is good to climb. And there are fruit trees, *lichis*, mangoes, papayas.'

'Are there any books?'

'Grandmother's books won't interest you. But I'll be bringing you books from Delhi, whenever I come to see you.'

I was beginning to look forward to the move. Changing houses had always been fun. Changing towns ought to be fun, too.

A few days before we left, I went to say goodbye to the Rani.

'I'm going away,' I said.

'How lovely!' said the Rani. 'I wish I could go away!'

'Why don't you?'

'They won't let me. They're afraid to let me out of the palace.'

'What are they afraid of, Your Highness?'

'That I might run away. Run away, far far away, to the land where the leopards are learning to pray.'

Gosh, I thought, she's really quite crazy....But then she was silent, and started smoking a small hookah.

She drew on the hookah, looked at me, and asked: 'Where is your mother?'

'I haven't one.'

'Everyone has a mother. Did yours die?'

'No. She went away.'

She drew her hookah again and then said, very sweetly, 'Don't go away. . . .'

'I must,' I said. 'It's because of the war.'

'What war? Is there a war on? You see, no one tells me anything.'

'It's between us and Hitler,' I said.

'And who is Hitler?'

'He's a German.'

'I knew a German once, Dr Schreinherr, he had beautiful hands.'

'Was he an artist?'

'He was a dentist.'

The Rani got up from her couch and accompanied me out on

33

to the balcony. When we looked down at the garden, we could see Dukhi weeding a flower-bed. Both of us gazed down at him in silence, and I wondered what the Rani would say if I asked her if she had ever been in love with the palace gardener. Ayah had told me it would be an insulting question; so I held my peace. But as I walked slowly down the spiral staircase, the Rani's voice came after me.

'Thank him,' she said. 'Thank him for the beautiful rose.'

Time Stops at Shamli

The Dehra Express usually drew into Shamli at about five o'clock in the morning, at which time the station would be dimly lit and the jungle across the tracks would just be visible in the faint light of dawn. Shamli is a small station at the foot of the Siwalik hills, and the Siwaliks lie at the foot of the Himalayas, which in turn lie at the feet of God.

The station, I remember, had only one platform, an office for the station-master, and a waiting-room. The platform boasted a tea-stall, a fruit vendor, and a few stray dogs; not much else was required, because the train stopped at Shamli for only five minutes before rushing on into the forests.

Why it stopped at Shamli, I never could tell. Nobody got off the train and nobody got in. There were never any coolies on the platform. But the train would stand there a full five minutes, and the guard would blow his whistle, and presently Shamli would be left behind and forgotten . . . .until I passed that way again.
. . .

I was paying my relations in Saharanpur an annual visit, when the night train stopped at Shamli. I was thirty-six at the time, and still single.

On this particular journey, the train came into Shamli just as I awoke from a restless sleep. The third class compartment was crowded beyond capacity, and I had been sleeping in an upright position, with my back to the lavatory door. Now someone was trying to get into the lavatory. He was obviously hardpressed for time.

'I'm sorry, brother,' I said, moving as much as I could do to one side.

He stumbled into the closet without bothering to close the door.

'Where are we now?' I asked the man sitting beside me. He

35

was smoking a strong aromatic *bidi*.

'Shamli station,' he said, rubbing the palm of a large calloused hand over the frosted glass of the window.

I let the window down and stuck my head out. There was a cool breeze blowing down the platform, a breeze that whispered of autumn in the hills. As usual there was no activity, except for the fruit-vendor walking up and down the length of the train with his basket of mangoes balanced on his head. At the tea-stall, a kettle was steaming, but there was no one to mind it. I rested my forehead on the window-ledge, and let the breeze play on my temples. I had been feeling sick and giddy but there was a wild sweetness in the wind that I found soothing.

'Yes,' I said to myself, 'I wonder what happens in Shamli, behind the station walls.' ·

My fellow passenger offered me a *bidi*. He was a farmer, I think, on his way to Dehra. He had a long, untidy, sad moustache.

We had been more than five minutes at the station, I looked up and down the platform, but nobody was getting on or off the train. Presently the guard came walking past our compartment.

'What's the delay?' I asked him.

'Some obstruction further down the line,' he said.

'Will we be here long?'

'I don't know what the trouble is. About half-an-hour, at the least.'

My neighbour shrugged, and, throwing the remains of his *bidi* out of the window, closed his eyes and immediately fell asleep. I moved restlessly in my seat, and then the man came out of the lavatory, not so urgently now, and with obvious peace of mind. I closed the door for him.

I stood up and stretched; and this stretching of my limbs seemed to set in motion a stretching of the mind, and I found myself thinking: 'I am in no hurry to get to Saharanpur, and I have always wanted to see Shamli, behind the station walls. If I get down now, I can spend the day here, it will be better than sitting in this train for another hour. Then in the evening I can catch the next train home.'

In those days I never had the patience to wait for second thoughts, and so I began pulling my small suitcase out from under the seat.

The farmer woke up and asked, 'What are you doing, brother?'

'I'm getting out,' I said.

He went to sleep again.

It would have taken at least fifteen minutes to reach the door, as people and their belongings cluttered up the passage; so I let my suitcase down from the window and followed it on to the platform.

There was no one to collect my ticket at the barrier, because there was obviously no point in keeping a man there to collect tickets from passengers who never came; and anyway, I had a through-ticket to my destination, which I would need in the evening.

I went out of the station and came to Shamli.

*

Outside the station there was a *neem* tree, and under it stood a *tonga* . The *tonga*-pony was nibbling at the grass at the foot of the tree. The youth in the front seat was the only human in sight; there were no signs of inhabitants or habitation. I approached the *tonga*, and the youth stared at me as though he couldn't believe his eyes.

'Where is Shamli?' I asked.

'Why, friend, this is Shamli,' he said.

I looked around again, but couldn't see any signs of life. A dusty road led past the station and disappeared in the forest.

'Does anyone live here?' I asked.

'I live here,' he said, with an engaging smile. He looked an amiable, happy-go-lucky fellow. He wore a cotton tunic and dirty white pyjamas.

'Where?' I asked.

'In my *tonga*, of course,' he said. 'I have had this pony five years now. I carry supplies to the hotel. But today the manager has not come to collect them. You are going to the hotel? I will take you.'

'Oh, so there's a hotel?'

'Well, friend, it is called that. And there are a few houses too, and some shops, but they are all about a mile from the station. If they were not a mile from here, I would be out of business.'

I felt relieved, but I still had the feeling of having walked into a town consisting of one station, one pony and one man.

'You can take me,' I said. 'I'm staying till this evening.'

He heaved my suitcase into the seat beside him, and I climbed in at the back. He flicked the reins and slapped his pony on the buttocks; and, with a roll and a lurch, the buggy moved off down the dusty forest road.

'What brings you here?' asked the youth.

'Nothing,' I said. 'The train was delayed, I was feeling bored, and so I got off.'

He did not believe that; but he didn't question me further. The sun was reaching up over the forest, but the road lay in the shadow of tall trees, eucalyptus, mango and *neem*.

'Not many people stay in the hotel,' he said. 'So it is cheap, you will get a room for five rupees.'

'Who is the manager?'

'Mr Satish Dayal. It is his father's property. Satish Dayal could not pass his exams or get a job, so his father sent him here to look after the hotel.'

The jungle thinned out, and we passed a temple, a mosque, a few small shops. There was a strong smell of burnt sugar in the air, and in the distance I saw a factory chimney: that, then, was the reason for Shamli's existence. We passed a bullock-cart laden with sugarcane. The road went through fields of cane and maize, and then, just as we were about to re-enter the jungle, the youth pulled his horse to a side road and the hotel came in sight.

It was a small white bungalow, with a garden in the front, banana tress at the sides, and an orchard of guava tress at the back. We came jingling up to the front verandah. Nobody appeared, nor was there any sign of life on the premises.

'They are all asleep,' said the youth.

I said, 'I'll sit in the verandah and wait.' I got down from the *tonga*, and the youth dropped my case on the verandah steps. Then he stood in front of me, smiling amiably, waiting to be paid.

'Well, how much?' I asked.

'As a friend, only one rupee.'

'That's too much,' I complained. 'This is not Delhi.'

'This is Shamli,' he said. 'I am the only *tonga* in Shamli. You may not pay me anything, if that is your wish. But then, I will not take you back to the station this evening, you will have to walk.'

I gave him the rupee. He had both charm and cunning, an effective combination.

'Come in the evening at about six,' I said.

'I will come,' he said, with an infectious smile, 'Don't worry.'

I waited till the *tonga* had gone round the bend in the road before walking up the verandah steps.

The doors of the house were closed, and there were no bells to ring. I didn't have a watch, but I judged the time to be a little past six o'clock. The hotel didn't look very impressive; the whitewash was coming off the walls, and the cane-chairs on the verandah were old and crooked. A stag's head was mounted over the front door, but one of its glass eyes had fallen out; I had often heard hunters speak of how beautiful an animal looked before it died, but how could anyone with a true love of the beautiful care for the stuffed head of an animal, grotesquely mounted, with no resemblance to its living aspect?

I felt too restless to take any of the chairs. I began pacing up and down the verandah, wondering if I should start banging on the doors. Perhaps the hotel was deserted; perhaps the *tonga*-driver had played a trick on me. I began to regret my impulsiveness in leaving the train. When I saw the manager I would have to invent a reason for coming to his hotel. I was good at inventing reasons. I would tell him that a friend of mine had stayed here some years ago, and that I was trying to trace him. I decided that my friend would have to be a little eccentric (having chosen Shamli to live in), that he had become a recluse, shutting himself off from the world; his parents—no, his sister— for his parents would be dead—had asked me to find him if I could; and, as he had last been heard of in Shamli, I had taken the opportunity to enquire after him. His name would be Major Roberts, retired.

I heard a tap running at the side of the building, and walking around, found a young man bathing at the tap. He was strong and well-built, and slapped himself on the body with great enthusiasm. He had not seen me approaching, and I waited until he had finished bathing and had began to dry himself.

'Hullo,' I said.

He turned at the sound of my voice, and looked at me for a few moments with a puzzled expression. he had a round, cheerful face and crisp black hair. He smiled slowly, but it was a more genuine smile than the *tonga*-driver's. So far I had met two people in Shamli, and they were both smilers; that should have cheered me, but it didn't. 'You have come to stay?' he asked, in a slow easy going voice.

'Just for the day,' I said. 'You work here?'

'Yes, my name is Daya Ram. The manager is asleep just now, but I will find a room for you.'

He pulled on his vest and pyjamas, and accompanied me back to the verandah. Here he picked up my suitcase and, unlocking a side door, led me into the house. We went down a passage way; then Daya Ram stopped at the door on the right, pushed it open, and took me into a small, sunny room that had a window looking out on the orchard. There was a bed, a desk, a couple of cane-chairs, and a frayed and faded red carpet.

'Is it all right?' said Daya Ram.

'Perfectly all right.'

'They have breakfast at eight o'clock. But if you are hungry, I will make something for you now.'

'No, it's all right. Are you the cook too.'

'I do everything here.'

'Do you like it.'

'No,' he said, and then added, in a sudden burst of confidence, 'There are no women for a man like me.'

'Why don't you leave, then?'

'I will,' he said, with a doubtful look on his face. 'I will leave....'

After he had gone I shut the door and went into the bathroom to bathe. The cold water refreshed me and made me feel one with the world. After I had dried myself, I sat on the bed, in front of the open window. A cool breeze, smelling of rain, came through the window and played over my body. I thought I saw a movement among the trees.

And getting closer to the window, I saw a girl on a swing. She was a small girl, all by herself, and she was swinging to and fro, and singing, and her song carried faintly on the breeze.

I dressed quickly, and left my room. The girl's dress was billowing in the breeze, her pigtails flying about. When she saw me approaching, she stopped swinging, and stared at me. I stopped a little distance away.

'Who are you?' she asked.

'A ghost.' I replied.

'You look like one,' she said.

I decided to take this as a compliment, as I was determined to make friends. I did not smile at her, because some children dislike adults who smile at them all the time.

'What's your name?' I asked.

'Kiran,' she said, 'I'm ten.'

'You are getting old.'

'Well, we all have to grow old one day. Aren't you coming any closer?'

'May I?' I asked.

'You may. You can push the swing.'

One pigtail lay across the girl's chest, the other behind her shoulder. She had a serious face, and obviously felt she had responsibilities; she seemed to be in a hurry to grow up, and I suppose she had no time for anyone who treated her as a child. I pushed the swing, until it went higher and higher, and then I stopped pushing, so that she came lower each time and we could talk.

'Tell me about the people who live here,' I said.

'There is Heera,' she said. 'He's the gardener. He's nearly a hundred. You can see him behind the hedges in the garden. You can't see him unless you look hard. He tells me stories, a new story every day. He's much better than the people in the hotel, and so is Daya Ram.'

'Yes, I met Daya Ram.'

'He's my bodyguard. He brings me nice things from the kitchen when no one is looking.'

'You don't stay here?'

'No, I live in another house, you can't see it from here. My father is the manager of the factory.'

'Aren't there any other children to play with?' I asked.

'I don't know any,' she said.

'And the people staying here?'

'Oh, *they*.' Apparently Kiran didn't think much of the hotel guests. 'Miss Deeds is funny when she's drunk. And Mr Lin is the *strangest*.'

'And what about the manager, Mr Dayal?'

'He's mean. And he gets frightened of slightest things. But Mrs Dayal is nice, she lets me take flowers home. But she doesn't talk

41

much.'

I was fascinated by Kiran's ruthless summing up of the guests. I brought the swing to a stand-still and asked, 'And what do you think of me?'

'I don't know as yet,' said Kiran quite seriously. 'I'll think about you.'

*

As I came back to the hotel, I heard the sound of a piano in one of the front rooms. I didn't know enough about music to be able to recognize the piece, but it had sweetness and melody, though it was played with some hesitancy. As I came nearer, the sweetness deserted the music, probably because the piano was out of tune.

The person at the piano had distinctive Mongolian features, and so I presumed he was Mr Lin. He hadn't seen me enter the room, and I stood beside the curtains of the door, watching him play. He had full round lips, and high slanting cheekbones. His eyes were large and round and full of melancholy. His long, slender fingers hardly touched the keys.

I came nearer; and then he looked up at me, without any show of surprise or displeasure, and kept on playing.

'What are you playing?' I asked.

'Chopin,' he said.

'Oh, yes. It's nice, but the piano is fighting it.'

'I know. This piano belonged to one of Kipling's aunts. It hasn't been tuned since the last century.'

'Do you live here?'

'No, I come from Calcutta,' he answered readily. 'I have some business here with the sugarcane people, actually, though, I am not a businessman.' He was playing softly all the time, so that our conversation was not lost in the music. 'I don't know anything about business. But I have to do something.'

'Where did you learn to play the piano?'

'In Singapore. A French lady taught me. She had great hopes of my becoming a concert pianist when I grow up. I would have toured Europe and America.'

'Why didn't you?'

'We left during the War, and I had to give up my lessons.'

'And why did you go to Calcutta?'

'My father is a Calcutta businessman. What do you do, and why do you come here?' he asked. 'If I am not being too inquisitive.'

Before I could answer, a bell rang, loud and continuously, drowning the music and conversation.

'Breakfast,' said Mr Lin.

A thin dark man, wearing glasses, stepped nervously into the room and peered at me in an anxious manner.

'You arrived last night?'

'That's right,' I said, 'I just want to stay the day. I think you're the manager?'

'Yes. Would you like to sign the register?'

I went with him past the bar and into the office. I wrote my name and Mussoorie address in the register, and the duration of my stay. I paused at the column marked 'Profession', thought it would be best to fill it with something and wrote 'Author'.

'You are here on business?' asked Mr Dayal.

'No, not exactly. You see, I'm looking for friend of mine who was heard of in Shamli, about three yea. · ago. I thought I'd make a few enquiries in case he's still here.

'What was his name? Perhaps he stayed here.'

'Major Roberts,' I said. 'An Anglo-Indian.'

'Well, you can look through the old registers after breakfast.'

He accompanied me into the dining-room. The establishment was really more of a boarding-house than a hotel, because Mr Dayal ate with his guests. There was a round mahogany dining-table in the centre of the room, and Mr Lin was the only one seated at it. Daya Ram hovered about with plates and trays. I took my seat next to Lin, and, as I did so, a door opened from the passage, and a woman of about thirty-five came in.

She had on a skirt and blouse, which accentuated a firm, well-rounded figure, and she walked on high-heels, with a rhythmical swaying of the hips. She had an uninteresting face, camouflaged with lipstick, rouge and powder—the powder so thick that is had become embedded in the natural lines of her face—but her figure compelled admiration.

'Miss Deeds,' whispered Lin.

There was a false note to her greeting.

'Hallo, everyone,' she said heartily, straining for effect. 'Why are you all so quiet? Has Mr Lin been playing the Funeral March again?' She sat down and continued talking. 'Really, we must have a dance or something to liven things up. You must know some good numbers Lin, after your experience of Singapore night-clubs. What's for breakfast? Boiled eggs. Daya Ram, can't you make an omelette for a change? I know you're not a professional cook, but you don't have to give us the same thing every day, and there's absolutely no reason why you should burn the toast. You'll have to do something about a cook, Mr Dayal.' Then she noticed me sitting opposite her. 'Oh, hallo,' she said, genuinely surprised. She gave me a long appraising look.

'This gentleman,' said Mr Dayal introducing me, 'is an author.'

'That's nice,' said Miss Deeds. 'Are you married?'

'No,' I said. 'Are you?'

'Funny, isn't it,' she said, without taking offence, 'No one in this house seems to be married.'

'I'm married,' said Mr Dayal.

'Oh, yes, of course,' said Miss Deeds. 'And what brings you to Shamli?' she asked, turning to me.

'I'm looking for a friend called Major Roberts.'

Lin gave an exclamation of surprise. I thought he had seen through my deception.

But another game had begun.

'I knew him,' said Lin. 'A great friend of mine.'

*

'Yes,' continued Lin. 'I knew him. A good chap, Major Roberts.'

Well, there I was, inventing people to suit my convenience, and people like Mr Lin started inventing relationships with them. I was too intrigued to try and discourage him. I wanted to see how far he would go.

'When did you meet him?' asked Lin, taking the initiative.

'Oh, only about three years back. Just before he disappeared. He was last heard of in Shamli.'

'Yes, I heard he was here,' said Lin. 'But he went away, when he thought his relatives had traced him. He went into the mountains near Tibet.'

'Did he?' I said, unwilling to be instructed further. 'What part

44

of the country? I come from the hills myself. I know the Mana and Niti passes quite well. If you have any idea of exactly where he went, I think I could find him.' I had the advantage in this exchange, because I was the one who had originally invented Roberts. Yet I couldn't bring myself to end his deception, probably because I felt sorry for him. A happy man wouldn't take the trouble of inventing friendships with people who didn't exist, he'd be too busy with friends who did

'You've had a lonely life, Mr Lin?' I asked.

'Lonely?' said Mr Lin, with forced incredulousness. 'I'd never been lonely till I came here a month ago. When I was in Singapore....'

'You never get any letters though, do you?' asked Miss Deeds suddenly.

Lin was silent for a moment. Then he said: 'Do you?'

Miss Deeds lifted her head a little, as a horse does when it is annoyed, and I thought her pride had been hurt; but then she laughed unobstrusively and tossed her head.

'I never write letters,' she said. 'My friends gave me up as hopeless years ago. They know it's no use writing to me, because they rarely get a reply. They call me the Jungle Princess.'

Mr Dayal tittered, and I found it hard to suppress a smile. To cover up my smile I asked, 'You teach here?'

'Yes, I teach at the girl's school,' she said with a frown. 'But don't talk to me about teaching. I have enough of it all day.'

'You don't like teaching?'

She gave an aggressive look. 'Should I?' she asked.

'Shouldn't you?' I said.

She paused, and then said, 'Who are you, anyway, the Inspector of Schools?'

'No,' said Mr Dayal who wasn't following very well, 'He's a journalist.'

'I've heard they are nosey,' said Miss Deeds.

Once again Lin interrupted to steer the conversation away from a delicate issue.

'Where's Mrs Dayal this morning?' asked Lin.

'She spent the night with our neighbours,' said Mr Dayal. 'She should be here after lunch.'

It was the first time Mrs Dayal had been mentioned. Nobody

spoke either well or ill of her; I suspected that she kept her distance from the others, avoiding familiarity. I began to wonder about Mrs Dayal.

*

Daya Ram came in from the verandah, looking worried.

'Heera's dog has disappeared,' he said. 'He thinks a leopard took it.'

Heera, the gardener was standing respectfully outside on the verandah steps. We all hurried out to him, firing questions which he didn't try to answer.

'Yes. It's a leopard,' said Kiran, appearing from behind Heera. 'It's going to come into the hotel,' she added cheerfully.

'Be quiet,' said Satish Dayal crossly.

'There are pug marks under the trees,' said Daya Ram.

Mr Dayal who seemed to know little about leopards or pug marks, said 'I will take a look', and led the way to the orchard, the rest of us trailing behind in an ill-assorted procession.

There were marks on the soft earth in the orchard (they could have been a leopard's) which went in the direction of the river bed. Mr Dayal paled a little and went hurrying back to the hotel. Heera returned to the front garden, the least excited, the most sorrowful. Everyone else was thinking of a leopard, but he was thinking of the dog.

I followed him, and watched him weeding the sunflower beds. His face wrinkled like a walnut, but his eyes were clear and bright. His hands were thin, and bony, but there was a deftness and power in the wrist and fingers, and the weeds flew fast from his spade. He had cracked, parchment-like skin. I could not help thinking of the gloss and glow of Daya Ram's limbs, as I had seen them when he was bathing, and wondered if Heera's had once been like that and if Daya Ram's would ever be like this, and both possibilities—or were they probabilities—saddened me. Our skin, I thought, is like the leaf of a tree, young and green and shiny; then it gets darker and heavier, sometimes spotted with disease, sometimes eaten away; then fading, yellow and red, then falling, crumbling into dust or feeding the flames of fire. I looked at my own skin, still smooth, not coarsened by labour; I thought of Kiran's fresh rose-tinted

46

complexion; Miss Deed's skin, hard and dry; Lin's pale taut skin, stretched tightly across his prominent cheeks and forehead; and Mr Dayal's grey skin, growing thick hair. And I wondered about Mrs Dayal and the kind of skin she would have.

'Did you have the dog for long?' I asked Heera.

He looked up with surprise, for he had been unaware of my presence.

'Six years, *sahib*,' he said. 'He was not a clever dog, but he was very friendly. He followed me home one day, when I was coming back from the bazaar. I kept telling him to go away, but he wouldn't. It was a long walk and so I began talking to him. I liked talking to him, and I have always talked with him, and we have understood each other. That first night, when I came home, I shut the gate between us. But he stood on the other side, looking at me with trusting eyes. Why did he have to look at me like that?'

'So you kept him?'

'Yes, I could never forget the way he looked at me. I shall feel lonely now, because he was my only companion. My wife and son died long ago. It seems I am to stay here forever, until everyone has gone, until there are only ghosts in Shamli. Already the ghosts are here. . . .'

I heard a light footfall behind me and turned to find Kiran. The bare-footed girl stood beside the gardener, and with her toes began to pull at the weeds.

'You are a lazy one,' said the old man. 'If you want to help me, sit down and use your hands.'

I looked at the girl's fair round face, and in her bright eyes I saw something old and wise; and I looked into the old man's wise eyes, and saw something forever bright and young. The skin cannot change the eyes; the eyes are the true reflection of a man's age and sensibilities; even a blind man has hidden eyes.

'I hope we shall find the dog,' said Kiran. 'But I would like a leopard. Nothing ever happens here.'

'Not now,' sighed Heera. 'Not now. . . . Why, once there was a band and people danced till morning, but now. . . .'

'I have always been here,' said Heera. 'I was here before Shamli.'

'Before the station?'

'Before there was a station, or a factory, or a bazaar. It was a

47

village then, and the only way to get here was by bullock-cart. Then a bus service was started, then the railway lines were laid and a station built, then they started the sugar factory, and for a few years Shamli was a town. But the jungle was bigger than the town. The rains were heavy and malaria was everywhere. People didn't stay long in Shamli. Gradually, they went back into the hills. Sometimes I too wanted to go back to the hills, but what is the use when you are old and have no one left in the world except a few flowers in a troublesome garden. I had to choose between the flowers and the hills, and I chose the flowers. I am tired now, and old, but I am not tired of flowers.'

I could see that his real world was the garden; there was more variety in his flower-beds than there was in the town of Shamli. Every month, every day, there were new flowers in the garden, but there were always the same people in Shamli.

I left Kiran with the old man, and returned to my room. It must have been about eleven o'clock.

*

I was facing the window when I heard my door being opened. Turning, I perceived the barrel of a gun moving slowly round the edge of the door. Behind the gun was Satish Dayal, looking hot and sweaty. I didn't know what his intentions were; so, deciding it would be better to act first and reason later, I grabbed a pillow from the bed and flung it in his face. I then threw myself at his legs and brought him crashing down to the ground.

When we got up, I was holding the gun. It was an old Enfield rifle, probably dating back to Afghan wars, the kind that goes off at the least encouragment.

'But—but—why?' stammered the dishevelled and alarmed Mr Dayal.

'I don't know,' I said menacingly. 'Why did you come in here pointing this at me?'

'I wasn't pointing it at you. It's for the leopard.'

'Oh, so you came into my room looking for a leopard? You have, I presume been stalking one about the hotel?' (By now I was convinced that Mr Dayal had taken leave of his senses and was hunting imaginary leopards.)

'No, no,' cried the distraught man, becoming more confused,

'I was looking for you. I wanted to ask you if you could use a gun. I was thinking we should go looking for the leopard that took Heera's dog. Neither Mr Lin nor I can shoot.'

'Your gun is not up-to-date.' I said. 'It's not at all suitable for hunting leopards. A stout stick would be more effective. Why don't we arm ourselves with *lathis* and make a general assault?'

I said this banteringly, but Mr Dayal took the idea quite seriously, 'Yes, yes,' he said with alacrity, 'Daya Ram has got one or two *lathis* in the godown. The three of us could make an expedition. I have asked Mr Lin but he says he doesn't want to have anything to do with leopards.'

'What about our Jungle Princess?' I said. 'Miss Deeds should be pretty good with a *lathi*.'

'Yes, yes.' said Mr Dayal humourlessly, 'but we'd better not ask her.'

Collecting Daya Ram and two *lathis,* we set off for the orchard and began following the pug marks through the trees. It took us ten minutes to reach the river bed, a dry hot rocky place; then we went into the jungle, Mr Dayal keeping well to the rear. The atmosphere was heavy and humid, and there was not a breath of air amongst the trees. When a parrot squawked suddenly, shattering the silence, Mr Dayal let out a startled exclamation and started for home.

'What was that?' he asked nervously.

'A bird,' I explained.

'I think we should go back now,' he said, 'I don't think the leopard's here.'

'You never know with leopards,' I said, 'They could be anywhere.'

Mr Dayal stopped away from the bushes. 'I'll have to go,' he said. 'I have a lot of work. You keep a *lathi* with you, and I'll send Daya Ram back later.'

'That's very thoughtful of you,' I said.

Daya Ram scratched his head and reluctantly followed his employer back through the trees. I moved on slowly, down the little-used path, wondering if I should also return. I saw two monkeys playing on the branch of a tree, and decided that there could be no danger in the immediate vicinity.

Presently I came to a clearing where there was a pool of fresh clear water. It was fed by a small stream that came suddenly, like a snake, out of the long grass. The water looked cool and inviting; laying down the *lathi* and taking off my clothes, I ran down the bank until I was waist-deep in the middle of the pool. I splashed about for some time, before emerging; then I lay on the soft grass and allowed the sun to dry my body. I closed my eyes and gave myself up to beautiful thoughts. I had forgotten all about leopards.

I must have slept for about half-an-hour because when I awoke, I found that Daya Ram had come back and was vigorously threshing about in the narrow confines of the pool. I sat up and asked him the time.

'Twelve o'clock,' he shouted, coming out of water, his dripping body all gold and silver in sunlight. 'They will be waiting for dinner.'

'Let them wait,' I said.

It was a relief to talk to Daya Ram, after the uneasy conversations in the lounge and dining-room.

'Dayal *sahib* will be angry with me.'

'I'll tell him we found the trail of the leopard, and that we went so far into the jungle that we lost our way. As Miss Deeds is so critical of the food, let her cook the meal.'

'Oh, she only talks like that,' said Daya Ram. 'Inside she is very soft. She is too soft in some ways.'

'She should be married.'

'Well, she would like to be. Only there is no one to marry her. When she came here she was engaged to be married to an English army captain; I think she loved him, but she is the sort of person who cannot help loving many men all at once, and the captain could not understand that—it is just the way she is made, I suppose. She is always ready to fall in love.'

'You seem to know,' I said.

'Oh, yes.'

We dressed and walked back to the hotel. In a few hours, I thought, the *tonga* will come for me and I will be back at the station; the mysterious charm of Shamli will be no more, but whenever I pass this way I will wonder about these people, about Miss Deeds and Lin and Mrs Dayal.

Mrs Dayal....She was the one person I had yet to meet; it was with some excitement and curiosity that I looked forward to meeting her; she was about the only mystery left to Shamli, now, and perhaps she would be no mystery when I met her. And yet....I felt that perhaps she would justify the impulse that made me get down from the train.

I could have asked Daya Ram about Mrs Dayal, and so satisfied my curiosity; but I wanted to discover her for myself. Half the day was left to me, and I didn't want my game to finish too early.

I walked towards the verandah, and the sound of the piano came through the open door.

'I wish Mr Lin would play something cheerful,' said Miss Deeds. 'He's obsessed with the Funeral March. Do you dance?'

'Oh no,' I said.

She looked disappointed. But when Lin left the piano, she went into the lounge and sat down on the stool. I stood at the door watching her, wondering what she would do. Lin left the room, somewhat resentfully.

She began to play an old song, which I remembered having heard in a film or on a gramophone record. She sang while she played, in a slightly harsh but pleasant voice:

> Rolling round the world
> Looking for the sunshine
> I know I'm going to find some day. . . .

Then she played *Am I blue?* and *Darling, Je Vous Aime Beaucoup*. She sat there singing in a deep husky voice, her eyes a little misty, her hard face suddenly kind and sloppy. When the dinner gong rang, she broke off playing, and shook off her sentimental mood, and laughed derisively at herself.

I don't remember that lunch. I hadn't slept much since the previous night and I was beginning to feel the strain of my journey. The swim had refreshed me, but it had also made me drowsy. I ate quite well, though, of rice and *kofta* curry, and then, feeling sleepy, made for the garden to find a shady tree.

There were some books on the shelf in the lounge, and I ran my eye over them in search of one that might condition sleep. But they were too dull to do even that. So I went into the garden, and there was Kiran on the swing, and I went to her tree and sat down on the grass.

'Did you find the leopard?' she asked.

51

'No,' I said, with a yawn.

'Tell me a story.'

'You tell me one,' I said.

'All right. Once there was a lazy man with long legs, who was always yawning and wanting to fall asleep. . . .'

I watched the swaying motions of the swing and the movements of the girl's bare legs, and a tiny insect kept buzzing about in front of my nose. . . .'and fall asleep, and the reason for this was that he liked to dream.' I blew the insect away, and the swing became hazy and distant, and Kiran was a blurred figure in the trees. . . .'liked to dream, and what do you think he dreamt about. . . .' dreamt about, dreamt about. . . .

*

When I awoke there was that cool rain-scented breeze blowing across the garden. I remember lying on the grass with my eyes closed, listening to the swishing of the swing. Either I had not slept long, or Kiran had been a long time on the swing; it was moving slowly now, in a more leisurely fashion, without much sound. I opened my eyes and saw that my arm was stained with the juice of the grass beneath me. Looking up, I expected to see Kiran's legs waving above me. But instead I saw dark slim feet, and above them the folds of a sari. I straightened up against the trunk of the tree to look closer at Kiran, but Kiran wasn't there, it was someone else in the swing, a young woman in a pink sari and with a red rose in her hair.

She had stopped the swing with her foot on the ground, and she was smiling at me.

It wasn't a smile you could see, it was a tender fleeting movement that came suddenly and was gone at the same time, and its going was sad. I thought of the other's smiles, just as I had thought of their skins: the *tonga*-driver's friendly, deceptive grin: Daya Ram's wide sincere smile; Miss Deed's cynical, derisive smile. And looking at Sushila, I knew a smile could never change. She had always smiled that way.

'You haven't changed,' she said.

I was standing up now, though still leaning against the tree for support. Though I had never thought much about the *sound* of her voice, it seemed as familiar as the sounds of yesterday.

'You haven't changed either,' I said. 'But where did you come from?' I wasn't sure yet if I was awake or dreaming.

She laughed, as she had always laughed at me.

'I came from behind the tree. The little girl has gone.'

'Yes I'm dreaming,' I said helplessly.

'But what brings you here?'

'I don't know. At least I didn't know when I came. But it must have been you. The train stopped at Shamli, and I don't know why, but I decided I would spend the day here, behind the station walls. You must be married now, Sushila.'

'Yes, I am married to Mr Dayal, the manager of the hotel. And what has been happening to you?'

'I am still a writer, still poor, and still living in Mussoorie.'

'When were you last in Delhi?' she asked. 'I don't mean Delhi, I mean at home.'

'I have not been to your home since you were there.'

'Oh, my friend,' she said, getting up suddenly and coming to me, 'I want to talk to you. I want to talk about our home and Sunil and our friends and all those things that are so far away now. I have been here two years, and I am already feeling old. I keep remembering our home, how young I was, how happy, and I am all alone with memories. But now *you* are here! It was a bit of magic, I came through the trees after Kiran had gone, and there you were, fast asleep under the tree. I didn't wake you then, because I wanted to see you wake up.'

'As I used to watch you wake up. . . .'

She was near me and I could look at her more closely. Her cheeks did not have the same freshness; they were a little pale, and she was thinned now, but her eyes were the same, smiling the same way. Her voice was the same. Her fingers, when she took my hand, were the same warm delicate fingers.

'Talk to me,' she said. 'Tell me about yourself.'

'You tell me,' I said.

'I am here,' she said. 'That is all there is about myself.'

'Then let us sit down and I'll talk.'

'Not here,' she took my hand and led me through the trees. 'Come with me.'

I heard the jingle of a *tonga*-bell and a faint shout, I stopped and laughed.

'My *tonga*,' I said, 'It has come to take me back to the station.'

'But you are not going,' said Sushila, immediately downcast.

'I will tell him to come in the morning,' I said. 'I will spend the night in your Shamli.'

I walked to the front of the hotel where the *tonga* was waiting. I was glad no one else was in sight. The youth was smiling at me in his most appealing manner.

'I'm not going today,' I said. 'Will you come tomorrow morning?'

'I can come whenever you like, friend. But you will have to pay for every trip, because it is a long way from the station even if my *tonga* is empty.'

'All right, how much?'

'Usual fare, friend, one rupee.'

I didn't try to argue but resignedly gave him the rupee. He cracked his whip and pulled on the reins, and the carriage moved off.

'If you don't leave tomorrow,' the youth called out after me, 'you'll never leave Shamli!'

I walked back to trees, but I couldn't find Sushila.

'Sushila where are you?' I called, but I might have been speaking to the trees, for I had no reply. There was a small path going through the orchard, and on the path I saw a rose petal. I walked a little further and saw another petal. They were from Sushila's red rose. I walked on down the path until I had skirted the orchard, and then the path went along the fringe of the jungle, past a clump of bamboos, and here the grass was a lush green as though it had been constantly watered. I was still finding rose petals. I heard the chatter of seven-sisters, and the call of hoopooe. The path bent to meet a stream, there was a willow coming down to the water's edge, and Sushila was waiting there.

'Why didn't you wait?' I said.

'I wanted to see if you were as good at following me as you used to be.'

'Well, I am,' I said, sitting down beside her on the grassy bank of the stream. 'Even if I'm out of practice.'

'Yes, I remember the time you climbed onto an apple tree to pick some fruit for me. You got up all right but then you couldn't come down again. I had to climb up myself and help you.'

'I don't remember that,' I said.

'Of course you do.'

'It must have been your other friend, Pramod.'

'I never climbed trees with Pramod.'

'Well, I don't remember.'

I looked at the little stream that ran past us. The water was no more than ankle-deep, cold and clear and sparkling, like the mountain-stream near my home. I took off my shoes, rolled up my trousers, and put my feet in water. Sushila's feet joined mine.

At first I had wanted to ask her about her marriage, whether she was happy or not, what she thought of her husband; but now I couldn't ask her these things, they seemed far away and of little importance. I could think of nothing she had in common with Mr Dayal; I felt that her charm and attractiveness and warmth could not have been appreciated, or even noticed, by that curiously distracted man. He was much older than her, of course; probably older than me; he was obviously not her choice but her parents'; and so far they were childless. Had there been children, I don't think Sushila would have minded Mr Dayal as her husband. Children would have made up for the absence of passion—or was there passion in Satish Dayal?....I remembered having heard that Sushila had been married to a man she didn't like; I remembered having shrugged off the news, because it meant she would never come my way again, and I have never yearned after something that has been irredeemably lost. But she *had* come my way again. And was she still lost? That was what I wanted to know....

'What do you do with yourself all day?' I asked.

'Oh, I visit the school and help with the classes. It is the only interest I have in this place. The hotel is terrible. I try to keep away from it as much as I can.'

'And what about the guests?'

'Oh, don't let us talk about them. Let us talk about ourselves. Do you have to go tomorrow?'

'Yes, I suppose so. Will you always be in this place?'

'I suppose so.'

That made me silent. I took her hand, and my feet churned up the mud at the bottom of the stream. As the mud subsided, I saw Sushila's face reflected in the water; and looking up at her again, into her dark eyes, the old yearning returned and I wanted to care for her and protect her, I wanted to take her away from that place, from sorrowful Shamli; I wanted her to live again. Of course, I had forgotten all about my poor finances, Sushila's family, and the shoes I wore, which were my last pair. The uplift I was experiencing in this meeting with Sushila, who had always, throughout her childhood and youth, bewitched me as no other had ever bewitched me, made me reckless and impulsive.

I lifted her hand to my lips and kissed her in the soft of the palm.

'Can I kiss you?' I said.

'You have just done so.'

'Can I kiss you?' I repeated.

'It is not necessary.'

I leaned over and kissed her slender neck. I knew she would like this, because that was where I had kissed her often before. I kissed her in the soft of the throat, where it tickled.

'It is not necessary,' she said, but she ran her fingers through my hair and let them rest there. I kissed her behind the ear then, and kept my mouth to her ear and whispered 'Can I kiss you?'

She turned her face to me so that we were deep in each other's eyes, and I kissed her again, and we put our arms around each other and lay together on the grass, with the water running over our feet; and we said nothing at all, simply lay there for what seemed like several years, or until the first drop of rain.

It was a big wet drop, and it splashed on Sushila's cheek, just next to mine, and ran down to her lips, so that I had to kiss her again. The next big drop splattered on the tip of my nose, and Sushila laughed and sat up. Little ringlets were forming on the stream where the rain-drops hit the water, and above us there was a pattering on the banana leaves.

'We must go,' said Sushila.

We started homewards, but had not gone far before it was raining steadily, and Sushila's hair came loose and streamed down her body. The rain fell harder, and we had to hop over pools and avoid the soft mud. Sushila's sari was plastered to her body, accentuating her ripe, thrusting breasts, and I was excited to passion, and pulled her beneath a big tree and crushed her in my arms and kissed her rain-kissed mouth. And then I thought she was crying, but I wasn't sure, because it might have been the rain-drops on her cheeks.

'Come away with me,' I said. 'Leave this place. Come away with me tomorrow morning. We will go somewhere where nobody will know us or come between us.'

She smiled at me and said, 'You are still a dreamer, aren't you?'

'Why can't you come?'

'I am married, it is as simple as that.'

'If it is that simple, you can come.'

'I have to think of my parents, too. It would break my father's heart if I were to do what you are proposing. And you are proposing it without a thought for the consequences.'

'You are too practical.' I said.

'If women were not practical, most marriages would be failures.'

'So your marriage is a success?'

'Of course it is, as a marriage. I am not happy and I do not love him, but neither am I so unhappy that I should hate him. Sometimes, for our own sakes, we have to think of the happiness of others. What happiness would *we* have living in hiding from everyone we once knew and cared for. Don't be a fool. I am always here and you can come to see me, and nobody will be made unhappy by it. But take me away and we will only have regrets.'

'You don't love me,' I said foolishly.

'That sad word *love*,' she said, and became pensive and silent.

I could say no more. I was angry again, and rebellious, and there was no one and nothing to rebel against. I could not understand someone who was afraid to break away from an unhappy existence lest that existence should become unhappier; I had always considered it an admirable thing to break away from security and respectability. Of course it is easier for a man to do this, a man can look after himself, he can do without neighbours and the approval of the local society. A woman, I reasoned, would do anything for love provided it was not at the price of security; for a woman loves security as much as a man loves independence.

'I must go back now,' said Suhsila. 'You follow a little later.'

'All you wanted to do was talk,' I complained.

She laughed at that, and pulled me playfully by the hair; then she ran out from under the tree, springing across the grass, and the wet mud flew up and flecked her legs. I watched her through the thin curtain of rain, until she reached the verandah. She turned to wave to me, and then skipped into the hotel. She was still young; but I was no younger.

*

The rain had lessened, but I didn't know what to do with myself. The hotel was uninviting, and it was too late to leave Shamli. If the grass hadn't been wet I would have preferred to sleep under a tree rather than return to the hotel to sit at that alarming dining-table.

I came out from under the trees and crossed the garden. But instead of making for the verandah I went round to the back of the hotel. Smoke issuing from the barred window of a back room told me I had probably found the kitchen. Daya Ram was inside, squatting in front of a stove, stirring a pot of stew. The stew smelt appetizing. Daya Ram looked up and smiled at me.

'I thought you must have gone,' he said.

'I'll go in the morning,' I said pulling myself upon an empty table. Then I had one of my sudden ideas and said, 'Why don't you come with me? I can find you a good job in Mussoorie. How much do you get paid here?'

'Fifty rupees a month. But I haven't been paid for three months.'

'Could you get your pay before tomorrow morning?'

'No, I won't get anything until one of the guests pays a bill. Miss Deeds owes about fifty rupees on whisky alone. She will pay up, she says, when the school pays her salary. And the school can't pay her until they collect the children's fees. That is how bankrupt everyone is in Shamli.'

'I see,' I said, though I didn't see. 'But Mr Dayal can't hold back your pay just because his guests haven't paid their bills.'

'He can, if he hasn't got any money.'

'I see,' I said, 'Anyway, I will give you my address. You can come when you are free.'

'I will take it from the register,' he said.

I edged over to the stove and, leaning over, sniffed at the stew. 'I'll eat mine now,' I said; and without giving Daya Ram a chance to object, I lifted a plate off the shelf, took hold of the stirring-spoon and helped myself from the pot.

'There's rice too.' said Daya Ram.

I filled another plate with rice and then got busy with my fingers. After ten minutes I had finished. I sat back comfortably in the hotel, in ruminative mood. With my stomach full I could take a more tolerant view of life and people. I could understand Sushila's apprehensions, Lin's delicate lying, and Miss Deed's aggressiveness. Daya Ram went out to sound the dinner-gong, and I trailed back to my room.

From the window of my room I saw Kiran running across the lawn, and I called to her, but she didn't hear me. She ran down the path and out of the gate, her pigtails beating against the wind.

The clouds were breaking and coming together again, twisting and spiralling their way across a violet sky. The sun was going down behind the Siwaliks. The sky there was blood-shot. The tall slim trunks of the eucalyptus tree were tinged with an orange glow; the rain had stopped, and the wind was a soft, sullen puff, drifting sadly through the trees. There was a steady drip of water from the eaves of the roof on to the window-sill. Then the sun went down behind the old, old hills, and I remembered my own hills, far beyond these.

The room was dark but I did not turn on the light. I stood near the window, listening to the garden. There was a frog warbling somewhere, and there was a sudden flap of wings overhead. Tomorrow morning I would go, and perhaps I would come back to Shamli one day, and perhaps not; I could always come here looking for Major Roberts, and, who knows, one day I might find him. What should he be like, this lost man? A romantic, a man with a dream, a man with brown skin and blue eyes, living in a hut on a snowy mountain-top, chopping wood and catching fish and swimming in cold mountain streams; a rough, free man with a kind heart and a shaggy beard, a man who owed allegiance to no one, who gave a damn for money and politics and cities, and civilizations, who was his own master, who lived at one with nature knowing no fear. But that was not Major Roberts—that was the man I wanted to be. He was not a Frenchman or an Englishman, he was me, a dream of myself. If only I could find Major Roberts.

*

59

When Daya Ram knocked on the door and told me the others had finished dinner, I left my room and made for the lounge. It was quite lively in the lounge. Satish Dayal was at the bar, Lin at the piano, and Miss Deeds in the centre of the room, executing a tango on her own. It was obvious she had been drinking heavily.

'All on credit,' complained Mr Dayal to me. 'I don't know when I'll be paid, but I don't dare to refuse her anything for fear she starts breaking up the hotel.'

'She could do that, too,' I said. 'It comes down without much encouragement.'

Lin began to play a waltz (I think it was waltz), and then I found Miss Deeds in front of me, saying 'Wouldn't you like to dance, old boy?'

'Thank you,' I said, somewhat alarmed. 'I hardly know how to.'

'Oh, come on, be a sport,' she said, pulling me away from the bar. I was glad Sushila wasn't present; she wouldn't have minded, but she'd have laughed as she always laughed when I made a fool of myself.

We went round the floor in what I suppose was waltz-time, though all I did was mark time to Miss Deeds' motions; we were not very steady—this because I was trying to keep her at arm's length, whilst she was determined to have me crushed to her bosom. At length Lin finished the waltz. Giving him a grateful look, I pulled myself free. Miss Deeds went over to the piano, leant right across it, and said, 'Play some lively, dear Mr Lin, play some hot stuff.'

To my surprise Mr Lin without so much as an expression of distaste or amusement, began to execute what I suppose was the frug or the jitterbug. I was glad she hadn't asked me to dance that one with her.

It all appeared very incongruous to me: Miss Deeds letting herself go in crazy abandonment, Lin playing the piano with great seriousness, and Mr Dayal watching from the bar with an anxious frown. I wondered what Sushila would have thought of them now.

Eventually Miss Deeds collapsed on the couch breathing heavily. 'Give me a drink,' she cried.

With the noblest of intentions I took her a glass of water. Miss

Deeds took a sip and made a face. 'What's this stuff?' she asked. 'It is different.'

'Water,' I said.

'No,' she said, 'now don't joke, tell me what it is.'

'It's water, I assure you,' I said.

When she saw that I was serious, her face coloured up, and I thought she would throw the water at me; but she was too tired to do this, and contented herself by throwing the glass over her shoulder. Mr Dayal made a dive for the flying glass, but he wasn't in time to rescue it, and it hit the wall and fell to pieces on the floor.

Mr Dayal wrung his hands. 'You'd better take her to her room,' he said, as though I were personally responsible for her behaviour just because I'd danced with her.

'I can't carry her alone,' I said, making an unsuccessful attempt at helping Miss Deeds up from the couch.

Mr Dayal called for Daya Ram, and the big amiable youth came lumbering into the lounge. We took an arm each and helped Miss Deeds, feet dragging, across the room. We got her to her room and on to her bed. When we were about to withdraw she said, 'Don't go, my dear, stay with me a little while.'

Daya Ram had discreetly slipped outside. With my hand on the door-knob I said, 'Which of us?'

'Oh, are there two of you,' said Miss Deeds, without a trace of disappointment.

'Yes, Daya Ram helped me carry you here.'

'Oh, and who are you?'

'I'm the writer. You danced with me, remember?'

'Of course. You dance divinely, Mr Writer. Do stay with me. Daya Ram can stay too if he likes.'

I hesitated, my hand on the door-knob. She hadn't opened her eyes all the time I'd been in the room, her arms hung loose, and one bare leg hung over the side of the bed. She was fascinating somehow, and desirable, but I was afraid of her. I went out of the room and quietly closed the door.

*

As I lay awake in bed I heard the jackal's 'pheau', the cry of fear, which it communicates to all the jungle when there is danger about, a leopard or a tiger. It was a weird howl, and between each note there was a kind of low gurgling. I switched off the light and peered through the closed window. I saw the jackal at the edge of the lawn. It sat almost vertically on its haunches, holding its head straight up to the sky, making the neighbourhood vibrate with the eerie violence of its cries. Then suddenly it started up and ran off into the trees.

Before getting back into bed I made sure the window was fast. The bull-frog was singing again, 'ing-ong, ing-ong', in some foreign language. I wondered if Sushila was awake too, thinking about me. It must have been almost eleven o'clock. I thought of Miss Deeds, with her leg hanging over the edge of the bed. I tossed restlessly, and then sat up. I hadn't slept for two nights but I was not sleepy. I got out of bed without turning on the light and, slowly opening my door, crept down the passage-way. I stopped at the door of Miss Deed's room. I stood there listening, but I heard only the ticking of the big clock that might have been in the room or somewhere in the passage. I put my hand on the door-knob, but the door was bolted. That settled the matter.

I would definitely leave Shamli the next morning. Another day in the company of these people and I would be behaving like them. Perhaps I was already doing so! I remembered the *tonga*-driver's words, 'Don't stay too long in Shamli or you will never leave!'

When the rain came, it was not with a preliminary patter or shower, but all at once, sweeping across the forest like a massive wall, and I could hear it in the trees long before it reached the house. Then it came crashing down on the corrugated roofing, and the hailstones hit the window panes with a hard metallic sound, so that I thought the glass would break. The sound of thunder was like the booming of big guns, and the lightning kept playing over the garden, at every flash of lightning I sighted the swing under the tree, rocking and leaping in the air as though some invisible, agitated being was sitting on it. I wondered about Kiran. Was she sleeping through all this, blissfully unconcerned, or was she lying awake in bed, starting at every clash of thunder, as I was; or was she up and about, exulting in the storm? I half expected to see her come running through the trees, through the rain, to stand on the swing with her hair blowing wild in the wind, laughing at the thunder and the angry skies. Perhaps I did see her, perhaps she was there. I wouldn't have been surprised if she were some forest nymph, living in the hole of a tree, coming out sometime to play in the garden.

A crash, nearer and louder than any thunder so far, made me sit up in the bed with a start. Perhaps lightning had struck the house. I turned on the switch, but the light didn't come on. A tree must have fallen across the line.

I heard voices in the passage, the voices of several people. I stepped outside to find out what had happened, and started at the appearance of a ghostly apparition right in front of me; it was Mr Dayal standing on the threshold in an oversized pyjama suit, a candle in his hand.

'I came to wake you,' he said. 'This storm.'

He had the irritating habit of stating the obvious.

'Yes, the storm,' I said. 'Why is everybody up?'

'The back wall has collapsed and part of the roof has fallen in. We'd better spend the night in the lounge, it is the safest room. This is a very old building,' he added apologetically.

'All right,' I said. 'I am coming.'

The lounge was lit by two candles; one stood over the piano, the other on a small table near the couch. Miss Deeds was on the couch, Lin was at the piano-stool, looking as though he would start playing Stravinsky any moment, and Mr Dayal was fussing about the room. Sushila was standing at a window, looking out at the stormy night. I went to the window and touched her, She didn't look round or say anything. The lightning flashed and her dark eyes were pools of smouldering fire.

'What time will you be leaving?' she said.

'The *tonga* will come for me at seven.'

'If I come,' she said. 'If I come with you, I will be at the station before the train leaves.'

'How will you get there?' I asked, and hope and excitement rushed over me again.

'I will get there,' she said. 'I will get there before you. But if I am not there, then do not wait, do not come back for me. Go on your way. It will mean I do not want to come. Or I will be there.'

'But are you sure?'

'Don't stand near me now. Don't speak to me unless you have to.' She squeezed my fingers, then drew her hand away. I sauntered over to the next window, then back into the centre of the room. A gust of wind blew through a cracked window-pane and put out the candle near the couch.

'Damn the wind,' said Miss Deeds.

The window in my room had burst open during the night, and there were leaves and branches strewn about the floor. I sat down on the damp bed, and smelt eucalyptus. The earth was red, as though the storm had bled it all night.

After a little while I went into the verandah with my suitcase, to wait for the *tonga*. It was then that I saw Kiran under the trees. Kiran's long black pigtails were tied up in a red ribbon, and she looked fresh and clean like the rain and the red earth. She stood looking seriously at me.

'Did you like the storm?' she asked.

'Some of the time,' I said. 'I'm going soon. Can I do anything for you?'

'Where are you going?'

'I'm going to the end of the world. I'm looking for Major Roberts, have you seen him anywhere?'

'There is no Major Roberts,' she said perceptively. 'Can I come with you to the end of the world?'

'What about your parents?'

'Oh, we *won't* take them.'

'They might be annoyed if you go off on your own.'

'I can stay on my own. I can go anywhere.'

'Well, one day I'll come back here and I'll take you everywhere and no one will stop us. Now is there anything else I can do for you?'

'I want some flowers, but I can't reach them,' she pointed to a hibiscus tree that grew against the wall. It meant climbing the wall to reach the flowers. Some of the red flowers had fallen during the night and were floating in a pool of water.

'All right,' I said and pulled myself up on the wall. I smiled down into Kiran's serious upturned face. 'I'll throw them to you and you can catch them.'

I bent a branch, but the wood was young and green, and I had to twist it several times before it snapped.

'I hope nobody minds,' I said, as I dropped the flowering

branch to Kiran.

'It's nobody's tree,' she said.

'Sure?'

She nodded vigorously. 'Sure, don't worry.'

I was working for her and she felt immensely capable of protecting me. Talking and being with Kiran, I felt a nostalgic longing for the childhood: emotions that had been beautiful because they were never completely understood.

'Who is your best friend?' I said.

'Daya Ram,' she replied. 'I told you so before.'

She was certainly faithful to her friends.

'And who is the second best?'

She put her finger in her mouth to consider the question; her head dropped sideways in concentration.

'I'll make you the second best,' she said.

I dropped the flowers over her head. 'That is so kind of you. I'm proud to be your second best.'

I heard the *tonga* bell, and from my perch on the wall saw the carriage coming down the driveway. 'That's for me,' I said. 'I must go now.'

I jumped down the wall. And the sole of my shoe came off at last.

'I knew that would happen,' I said.

'Who cares for shoes,' said Kiran.

'Who cares,' I said.

I walked back to the verandah, and Kiran walked beside me, and stood in front of the hotel while I put my suitcase in the *tonga*.

'You nearly stayed one day too late,' said the *tonga*-driver. 'Half the hotel has come down, and tonight the other half will come down.'

I climbed into the back seat. Kiran stood on the path, gazing intently at me.

'I'll see you again,' I said.

'I'll see you in Iceland or Japan,' she said. 'I'm going everywhere.'

'Maybe,' I said, 'maybe you will.'

We smiled, knowing and understanding each other's importance. In her bright eyes I saw something old and wise. The *tonga*-driver cracked his whip, the wheels cracked, the carriage rattled down the path. We kept waving to each other. In Kiran's hand was a spring of hibiscus. As she waved, the blossoms fell apart and danced a little in breeze.

*

Shamli station looked the same as it had the day before. The same train stood at the same platform, and the same dogs prowled beside the fence. I waited on the platform until the bell clanged for the train to leave, but Sushila did not come.

Somehow, I was not disappointed. I had never really expected her to come. Unattainable, Sushila would always be more bewitching and beautiful than if she were mine.

Shamli would always be there. And I could always come back, looking for Major Roberts.

Most Beautiful

I don't quite know why I found that particular town so heartless, perhaps because of its crowded, claustrophobic atmosphere, its congested and insanitary lanes, its weary people. . . .One day I found the children of the bazaar tormenting a deformed retarded boy.

About a dozen boys, between the ages of eight and fourteen, were jeering at the retard, who was making things worse for himself by confronting the gang and shouting abuses at them. The boy was twelve or thirteen, judging by his face; but had the height of an eight or nine-year-old. His legs were thick, short and bowed. He had a small chest but his arms were long, making him rather ape-like in his attitude. His forehead and cheeks were pitted with the scars of small-pox. He was ugly by normal standards, and the gibberish he spoke did nothing to discourage his tormentors. They threw mud and stones at him, while keeping well out of his reach. Few can be more cruel than a gang of schoolboys in high spirits.

I was an uneasy observer of the scene. I felt that I ought to do something to put a stop to it, but lacked the courage to interfere. It was only when a stone struck the boy on the face, cutting open his cheek, that I lost my normal discretion and ran in amongst the boys, shouting at them and clouting those I could reach. They scattered like defeated soldiery.

I was surprised at my own daring, and rather relieved when the boys did not return. I took the frightened, angry boy by the hand, and asked him where he lived. He drew away from me, but I held on to his fat little fingers and told him I would take him home. He mumbled something incoherent and pointed down a narrow line. I led him away from the bazaar.

I said very little to the boy because it was obvious that he had some defect of speech. When he stopped outside a door set in a high wall, I presumed that we had come to his house.

The door was opened by a young woman. The boy immediately threw his arms around her and burst into tears. I had not been prepared for the boy's mother. Not only did she look perfectly normal physically, but she was also strikingly handsome. She must have been about thirty-five.

She thanked me for bringing her son home, and asked me into the house. The boy withdrew into a corner of the sitting-room, and sat on his haunches in gloomy silence, his bow legs looking even more grotesque in this posture. His mother offered me tea, but I asked for a glass of water. She asked the boy to fetch it, and he did so, thrusting the glass into my hands without looking me in the face.

'Suresh is my only son,' she said. 'My husband is disappointed in him, but I love my son. Do you think he is very ugly?'

'Ugly is just a word,' I said. 'Like beauty. They mean different things to different people. What did the poet say? "Beauty is truth, truth is beauty." But if beauty and truth are the same thing why have different words? There are no absolutes except birth and death.'

The boy squatted down at her feet, cradling his head in her lap. With the end of her sari, she began wiping his face.

'Have you tried teaching him to talk properly?' I asked.

'He has been like this since childhood. The doctors can do nothing.'

While we were talking the father came in, and the boy slunk away to the kitchen. The man thanked me curtly for bringing the boy home, and seemed at once to dismiss the whole matter from his mind. He seemed preoccupied with business matters. I got the impression that he had long since resigned himself to having a deformed son, and his early disappointment had changed to indifference. When I got up to leave, his wife accompanied me to the front door.

'Please do not mind if my husband is a little rude,' she said. 'His business is not going too well. If you would like to come again, please do. Suresh does not meet many people who treat him like a normal person.'

I knew that I wanted to visit them again—more out of sympathy for the mother than out of pity for the boy. But I realized that she was not interested in me personally, except as a possible mentor for her son.

After about a week I went to the house again.

Suresh's father was away on a business trip, and I stayed for lunch. The boy's mother made some delicious *parathas* stuffed with ground raddish, and served it with pickle and curds. If Suresh ate like an animal, gobbling his food, I was not far behind him. His mother encouraged him to overeat. He was morose and uncommunicative when he ate, but when I suggested that he come with me for a walk, he looked up eagerly. At the same time a look of fear passed across his mother's face.

'Will it be all right?' she asked. 'You have seen how other children treat him. That day he slipped out of the house without telling anyone.'

'We won't go towards the bazaar,' I said. 'I was thinking of a walk in the fields.'

Suresh made encouraging noises and thumped the table with his fists to show that he wanted to go. Finally his mother consented, and the boy and I set off down the road.

He could not walk very fast because of his awkward legs, but this gave me a chance to point out to him anything that I thought might arouse his interest—parrots squabbling in a banyan tree, buffaloes wallowing in a muddy pond, a group of hermaphrodite musicians strolling down the road. Suresh took a keen interest in the hermaphrodites, perhaps because they were grotesque in their own way: tall, masculine-looking people dressed in women's garments, ankle-bells jingling on their heavy feet, and their long, gaunt faces made up with rouge and mascara. For the first time, I heard Suresh laugh. Apparently he had discovered that there were human beings even odder than he. And like any human being, he lost no time in deriding them.

'Don't laugh,' I said. 'They were born that way, just as you were born the way you are.'

But he did not take me seriously and grinned, his wide mouth revealing surprisingly strong teeth.

We reached the dry river-bed on the outskirts of the town, and, crossing it entered a field of yellow mustard flowers. The mustard stretched away towards the edge of a sub-tropical forest. Seeing trees in the distance, Suresh began to run towards them, shouting and clapping his hands. He had never been out of town before. The courtyard of his house and, occasionally, the road to the bazaar, were all that he had seen of the world. Now the trees beckoned him.

We found a small stream running through the forest and I took off my clothes and leapt into the cool water, inviting Suresh to join me. He hesitated about taking off his clothes; but after watching me for a while, his eagerness to join me overcame his self-consciousness, and he exposed his misshapen little body to the soft spring sunshine.

He waded clumsily towards me. The water which came only to my knees reached up to his chest.

'Come, I'll teach you, to swim,' I said. And lifting him up from the waist, I held him afloat. He spluttered and thrashed around, but stopped struggling when he found that he could stay afloat.

Later, sitting on the banks of the stream, he discovered a small turtle sitting over a hole in the ground in which it had laid the eggs. He had never watched a turtle before, and watched it in fascination, while it drew its head into its shell and then thrust it out again with extreme circumspection. He must have felt that the turtle resembled him in some respects, with its squat legs, rounded back, and tendency to hide its head from the world.

After that, I went to the boy's house about twice a week, and we nearly always visited the stream. Before long Suresh was able to swim a short distance. Knowing how to swim—this was something the bazaar boys never learnt—gave him a certain confidence, made his life something more than a one-dimensional existence.

The more I saw Suresh, the less conscious was I of his deformities. For me, he was fast becoming the norm; while the children of the bazaar seemed abnormal in their very similarity to each other. That he was still conscious of his ugliness—and how could he ever cease to be—was made clear to me about two months after our first meeting.

We were coming home through the mustard fields, which had turned from yellow to green, when I noticed that we were being followed by a small goat. It appeared to have been separated from its mother, and now attached itself to us. Though I tried driving the kid away, it continued tripping along at out heels, and when Suresh found that it persisted in accompanying us, he picked up and took it home.

The kid became his main obsession during the next few days.

He fed it with his own hands and allowed it to sleep at the foot of his bed. It was a pretty little kid, with fairy horns and an engaging habit of doing a hop, skip and jump when moving about the house. Everyone admired the pet, and the boy's mother and I both remarked on how pretty it was.

His resentment against the animal began to show when others started admiring it. He suspected that they found it better-looking than its owner. I remember finding him squatting in front of a low mirror, holding the kid in his arms, and studying their reflections in the glass. After a few minutes of this, Suresh thrust the goat away. When he noticed that I was watching him, he got up and left the room without looking at me.

Two days later, when I called at the house, I found his mother looking very upset. I could see that she had been crying. But she seemed relieved to see me, and took me into the sitting room. When Suresh saw me, he got up from the floor and ran to the verandah.

'What's wrong?' I asked.

'It was the little goat,' she said. 'Suresh killed it.'

She told me how Suresh, in a sudden and uncontrollable rage, had thrown a brick at the kid, breaking its skull. What had upset her more than the animal's death was the fact that Suresh had shown no regret for what he had done.

'I'll talk to him,' I said, and went out on the verandah; but the boy had disappeared.

'He must have gone to the bazaar,' said his mother anxiously. 'He does that when he's upset. Sometimes I think he likes to be teased and beaten.'

He was not in the bazaar. I found him near the stream, lying flat on his belly in the soft mud, chasing tadpoles with a stick.

'Why did you kill the goat?' I asked.

He shrugged his shoulders.

'Did you enjoy killing it?'

He looked at me and smiled and nodded his head vigorously.

'How very cruel,' I said. But I did not mean it. I knew that his cruelty was no different from mine or anyone else's; only his was an untrammelled cruelty, primitive, as yet undisguised by civilizing restraints.

He took a pen-knife from his shirt pocket opened it, and held it out to me by the blade. He pointed to his bare stomach and motioned me to thrust the blade into his belly. He had such a mournful look on his face (the result of having offended me and not in remorse for the goat-sacrifice) that I had to burst out laughing.

'You are a funny fellow,' I said, taking the knife from him and throwing it into the stream. 'Come, let's have a swim.'

We swam all afternoon, and Suresh went home smiling. His mother and I conspired to keep the whole affair a secret from his father—who had not in any case, been aware of the goat's presence.

Suresh seemed quite contented during the following weeks. And then I received a letter offering me a job in Delhi and I knew that I would have to take it, as I was earning very little by my writing at the time.

The boy's mother was disappointed, even depressed, when I told her I would be going away. I think she had grown quite fond of me. But the boy, always unpredictable, displayed no feeling at all. I left a little hurt by his apparent indifference. Did our weeks of companionship mean nothing to him ? I told myself that he probably did not realize that he might never see me again.

On the evening my train was to leave, I went to the house to say goodbye. The boy's mother made me promise to write to them, but Suresh seemed cold and distant, and refused to sit near me or take my hand. He made me feel that I was an outsider again—one of the mob throwing stones at odd and frightening people.

At eight o'clock that evening I entered a third-class compartment and, after a brief scuffle with several other travellers, succeeded in securing a seat near a window. It enabled me to look down the length of the platform.

The guard had blown his whistle and the train was about to leave, when I saw Suresh standing near the station turnstile, looking up and down the platform.

'Suresh!' I shouted and he heard me and came hobbling along the platform. He had run the gauntlet of the bazaar during the busiest hour of the evening.

'I'll be back next year.' I called.

The train had begun moving out of the station, and as I waved to Suresh, he broke into a stumbling run, waving his arms in frantic, restraining gestures.

I saw him stumble against someone's bedding-roll and fall sprawling on the ground. The engine picked up speed and the platform receded.

And that was the last I saw of Suresh, lying alone on the crowded platform, alone in the great grey darkness of the world, crooked and bent and twisted—the most beautiful boy in the world.

The Last Truck Ride

A horn blared, shattering the silence of the mountains, and a truck came round the bend in the road. A herd of goats scattered to left and right.

The goat-herds cursed as a cloud of dust enveloped them, and then the truck had left them behind and was rattling along the stony, unpaved hill road.

At the wheel of the truck, stroking his gray moustache, sat Pritam Singh, a turbaned Sikh. It was his own truck. He did not allow anyone else to drive it. Every day he made two trips to the limestone quarries, carrying truckloads of limestone back to the depot at the bottom of the hill. He was paid by the trip, and he was always anxious to get in two trips every day.

Sitting beside him was Nathu, his cleaner-boy.

Nathu was a sturdy boy, with a round cheerful face. It was difficult to guess his age. He might have been twelve or he might have been fifteen—he did not know himself, since no one in his village had troubled to record his birthday—but the hard life he led probably made him look older than his years. He belonged to the hills, but his village was far away, on the next range.

Last year the potato crop had failed. As a result there was no money for salt, sugar, soap and flour—and Nathu's parents and small brothers and sisters couldn't live entirely on the onions and artichokes which were about the only crops that had survived the drought. There had been no rain that summer. So Nathu waved good-bye to his people and came down to the town in the valley to look for work. Someone directed him to the limestone depot. He was too young to work at the quarries, breaking stones and loading them on the trucks; but Pritam Singh, one of the older drivers, was looking for someone to clean and look after his truck. Nathu looked like a bright, strong boy, and he was taken on—at ten rupees a day.

That had been six months ago, and now Nathu was an experienced hand at looking after trucks, riding in them and even sleeping in them. He got on well with Pritam Singh, the grizzled, fifty-year-old Sikh, who had well-to-do sons in the Punjab, but whose sturdy independence kept him on the road in his battered old truck.

Pritam Singh pressed hard on his horn. Now there was no one on the road—no animals, no humans—but Pritam was fond of his horn and liked blowing it. It was music to his ears.

'One more year on this road,' said Pritam. 'Then I'll sell my truck and retire.'

'Who will buy this truck?' said Nathu. 'It will retire before you do.'

'Don't be cheeky, boy. She's only twenty-years-old—there's still a few years left in her! And as though to prove it, he blew his horn again. Its strident sound echoed and re-echoed down the mountain gorge. A pair of wild fowl, disturbed by the noise, flew out from the bushes and glided across the road in front of the truck.

Pritam Singh's thoughts went to his dinner.

'Haven't had a good meal for days,' he grumbled.

'Haven't had a good meal for weeks,' said Nathu, although he looked quite well-fed.

'Tomorrow I'll give you dinner,' said Pritam. '*Tandoori* chicken and *pilau* rice.'

'I'll believe it when I see it,' said Nathu.

Pritam Singh sounded his horn again before slowing down. The road had become narrow and precipitous, and trotting ahead of them was a train of mules.

As the horn blared, one mule ran forward, one ran backwards. One went uphill, one went downhill. Soon there were mules all over the place.

'You can never tell with mules,' said Pritam, after he had left them behind.

The hills were bare and dry. Much of the forest had long since disappeared. Just a few scraggy old oaks still grew on the steep hillside. This particular range was rich in limestone, and the hills were scarred by quarrying.

'Are your hills as bare as these?' asked Pritam.

'No, they have not started blasting there as yet,' said Nathu. 'We still have a few trees. And there is a walnut tree in front of our house, which gives us two baskets of walnuts every year.'

'And do you have water?'

'There is a stream at the bottom of the hill. But for the fields, we have to depend on the rainfall. And there was no rain last year.'

'It will rain soon.' said Pritam. 'I can smell rain. It is coming from the north.'

'It will settle the dust.'

The dust was everywhere. The truck was full of it. The leaves of the shrubs and few trees were thick with it. Nathu could feel the dust near his eyelids and on his lips.

As they approached the quarries, the dust increased—but it was a different kind of dust now, whiter, stinging the eyes, irritating the nostrils—limestone dust, hanging in the air.

The blasting was in progress.

Pritam Singh brought the truck to a halt.

'Let's wait a bit,' he said.

They sat in silence, staring through the windscreen at the scarred cliffs about a hundred yards down the road. There were no signs of life around them.

Suddenly, the hillside blossomed outwards, followed by a sharp crack of explosives. Earth and rock hurtled down the hillside.

Nathu watched in awe as shrubs and small trees were flung into the air. It always frightened him—not so much the sight of the rocks bursting asunder, but the trees being flung aside and destroyed. He thought of his own trees at home—the walnut, the pines—and wondered if one day they would suffer the same fate, and whether the mountains would all become a desert like this particular range. No trees, no grass, no water—only the choking dust of the limestone quarries.

Pritam Singh pressed hard on his horn again, to let the people at the site know he was coming. Soon they were parked outside a small shed, where the contractor and the overseer were sipping cups of tea. A short distance away some labourers were hammering at chunks of rock, breaking them up into manageable blocks. A pile of stones stood ready for loading, while the rock that had just been blasted lay scattered about the hillside.

'Come and have a cup of tea,' called out the contractor.

'Get on with the loading,' said Pritam. 'I can't hang about all afternoon. There's another trip to make—and it gets dark early these days.'

But he sat down on a bench and ordered two cups of tea from the stall-owner. The overseer strolled over to the group of labourers and told them to start loading. Nathu let down the grid at the back of the truck.

Nathu stood back while the men loaded the truck with limestone rocks. He was glad that he was chubby: thin people seemed to feel the cold much more—like the contractor, a skinny fellow who was shivering in his expensive overcoat.

To keep himself warm, Nathu began helping the labourers with the loading.

'Don't expect to be paid for that,' said the contractor, for whom every extra paisa spent was a paisa off his profits.

'Don't worry,' said Nathu, 'I don't work for contractors. I work for Pritam Singh.'

'That's right,' called out Pritam. 'And mind what you say to Nathu—he's nobody's servant!'

It took them almost an hour to fill the truck with stones. The contractor wasn't happy until there was no space left for a single stone. Then four of the six labourers climbed on the pile of stones. They would ride back to the depot on the truck. The contractor, his overseer, and the others would follow by jeep.

'Let's go!' said Pritam, getting behind the steering wheel. 'I want to be back here and then home by eight o'clock. I'm going to a marriage party tonight!'

Nathu jumped in beside him, banging his door shut. It never closed properly unless it was slammed really hard. But it opened at a touch. Pritam always joked that his truck was held together with the selotape.

He was in good spirits. He started his engine, blew his horn, and burst into a song as the truck started out on the return journey.

The labourers were singing too, as the truck swung round the sharp bends of the winding mountain road. Nathu was feeling quite dizzy. The door beside him rattled on its hinges.

'Not so fast,' he said.

'Oh,' said Pritam, 'And since when did you become nervous about fast driving?'

'Since today,' said Nathu.

'And what's wrong with today?'

'I don't know. It's just that kind of day, I suppose.'

'You are getting old,' said Pritam. 'That's your trouble.'

'Just wait till you get to be my age,' said Nathu.

'No more cheek,' said Pritam, and stepped on the accelerator and drove faster.

As they swung round a bend, Nathu looked out of his window. All he saw was the sky above and the valley below. They were very near the edge. But it was always like that on this narrow road.

After a few more hairpin bends, the roads started descending steeply to the valley.

'I'll just test the brakes,' said Pritam and jammed down on them so suddenly that one of the labourers almost fell off at the back. They called out in protest.

'Hang on!' shouted Pritam. 'You're nearly home!'

'Don't try any short cuts,' said Nathu.

Just then a stray mule appeared in the middle of the road. Pritam swung the steering wheel over to his right; but the road turned left, and the truck went straight over the edge.

As it tipped over, hanging for a few seconds on the edge of the cliff, the labourers leapt from the back of the truck.

The truck pitched forward, and as it struck a rock outcrop, the door near Nathu burst open. He was thrown out.

Then the truck hurtled forward, bouncing over the rocks, turning over on its side and rolling over twice before coming to rest against the trunk of a scraggy old oak tree. Had it missed the tree, the truck would have plunged a few hundred feet down to the bottom of the gorge.

Two labourers sat on the hillside, stunned and badly shaken. The other two had picked themselves up and were running back to the quarry for help.

Nathu had landed in a bed of nettles. He was smarting all over, but he wasn't really hurt.

His first impulse was to get up and run back with the labourers. Then he realized that Pritam was still in the truck. If he wasn't dead, he would certainly be badly injured.

Nathu skidded down the steep slope, calling out 'Pritam, Pritam, are you all right?'

There was no answer.

Then he saw Pritam's arm and half his body jutting out of the open door of the truck. It was a strange position to be in, half in and half out. When Nathu came nearer, he saw Pritam was jammed in the driver's seat, held there by the steering wheel which was pressed hard against his chest. Nathu thought he was dead. But as he was about to turn away and clamber back up the hill, he saw Pritam open one blackened swollen eye. It looked straight up at Nathu.

'Are you alive?' whispered Nathu, terrified.

'What do you think?' muttered Pritam.

He closed his eye again.

When the contractor and his men arrived, it took them almost an hour to get Pritam Singh out of the wreckage of his truck, and another hour to get him to a hospital in the town. He had a broken collarbone, a dislocated shoulder, and several fractured ribs. But the doctors said he was repairable—which was more than could be said for his truck.

'The truck's finished,' said Pritam, when Nathu came to see him a few days later. 'Now I'll have to go home and live with my sons. But you can get work on another truck.'

'No,' said Nathu. I'm going home too.'

'And what will you do there?'

'I'll work on the land. It's better to grow things on the land than to blast things out of it.'

They were silent for some time.

'Do you know something?' said Pritam finally. 'But for that tree, the truck would have ended up at the bottom of the hill and I wouldn't be here, all bandaged up and talking to you. It was the tree that saved me. Remember that, boy.'

'I'll remember,' said Nathu.

The Fight

Ranji had been less than a month in Rajpur when he discovered the pool in the forest. It was the height of summer, and his school had not yet opened; and, having as yet made no friends in this semi-hill-station, he wandered about a good deal by himself into the hills and forests that stretched away interminably on all sides of the town. It was hot, very hot, at that time of the year, and Ranji walked about in his vest and shorts, his brown feet white with the chalky dust that flew up from the ground. The earth was parched, the grass brown, the trees listless, hardly stirring, waiting for a cool wind or a refreshing shower of rain.

It was on such a day—a hot, tired day—that Ranji found the pool in the forest. The water had a gentle translucency, and you could see the smooth round pebbles at the bottom of the pool. A small stream emerged from a cluster of rocks to feed the pool. During the monsoon, this stream would be a gushing torrent, cascading down from the hills, but during the summer it was barely a trickle. The rocks, however, held the water in the pool, and it did not dry up like the pools in the plains.

When Ranji saw the pool, he did not hesitate to get into it. He had often gone swimming, alone or with friends, when he had lived with his parents in a thirsty town in the middle of the Rajputana desert. There, he had known only sticky, muddy pools, where buffaloes wallowed and women washed clothes. He had never seen a pool like this—so clean and cold and inviting. He threw off all his clothes, as he had done when he went swimming in the plains, and leapt into the water. His limbs were supple, free of any fat, and his dark body glistened in patches of sunlit water.

*

The next day he came again to quench his body in the cool

80

waters of the forest pool. He was there for almost an hour, sliding in and out of the limpid green water, or lying stretched out on the smooth yellow rocks in the shade of broad-leaved *sal* trees. It was while he lay thus, naked on a rock, that he noticed another boy standing a little distance away, staring at him in a rather hostile manner. The other boy was a little older than Ranji, taller, thick-set with a broad nose and thick, red lips. He had only just noticed Ranji, and he stood at the edge of the pool, wearing a pair of bathing shorts, waiting for Ranji to explain himself.

When Ranji did not say anything, the other called out, 'What are you doing here, Mister?'

Ranji, who was prepared to be friendly, was taken aback at the hostility of the other's tone.

'I am swimming,' he replied. 'Why don't you join me?'

'I always swim alone,' said the other. 'This is my pool, I did not invite you here. And why are you not wearing any clothes?'

'It is not your business if I do not wear clothes. I have nothing to be ashamed of.'

'You skinny fellow, put on your clothes.'

'Fat fool, take yours off.'

This was too much for the stranger to tolerate. He strode up to Ranji, who still sat on the rock and, planting his broad feet firmly on the sand, said (as though this would settle the matter once and for all), 'Don't you know I am a Punjabi? I do not take replies from villagers like you!'

'So you like to fight with villagers?' said Ranji. 'Well, I am not a villager: I am a Rajput!'

'I am a Punjabi!'

'I am a Rajput!'

They had reached an impasse. One had said he was a Punjabi, the other had proclaimed himself a Rajput. There was little else that could be said.

'You understand that I am a Punjabi?' said the stranger, feeling that perhaps this information had not penetrated Ranji's head.

'I have heard you say it three times,' replied Ranji.

'Then why are you not running away?'

'I am waiting for *you* to run away!'

'I will have to beat you,' said the stranger, assuming a violent attitude, showing Ranji the palm of his hand.

'I am waiting to see you do it,' said Ranji.

'You will see me do it,' said the other boy.

Ranji waited. The other boy made a strange, hissing sound. They stared each other in the eye for almost a minute. Then the Punjabi boy slapped Ranji across the face with all the force he could muster. Ranji staggered, feeling quite dizzy. There were thick red finger-marks on his cheek.

'There you are!' exclaimed his assailant. 'Will you be off now?'

For answer, Ranji swung his arm up and pushed a hard, bony fist into the other's face.

And then they were at each other's throats, swaying on the rock, tumbling on to the sand, rolling over and over, their legs and arms locked in a desperate, violent struggle. Gasping and cursing, clawing and slapping, they rolled right into the shallows of the pool.

Even in the water the fight continued as, spluttering and covered with mud, they groped for each other's heads and throats. But after five minutes of frenzied, unscientific struggle, neither boy had emerged victorious. Their bodies heaving with exhaustion, they stood back from each other, making tremendous efforts to speak.

'Now—now do you realize—I am a Punjabi?' gasped the stranger.

'Do you know I am a Rajput?' said Ranji with difficulty.

They gave a moment's consideration to each other's answers, and in that moment of silence there was only their heavy breathing and the rapid beating of their hearts.

'Then you will not leave the pool?' said the Punjabi boy.

'I will not leave it,' said Ranji.

'Then we shall have to continue the fight,' said the other.

'All right,' said Ranji.

But neither boy moved, neither took the initiative.

Then the Punjabi boy had an inspiration.

'We will continue the fight tomorrow,' he said. 'If you dare to come here again tomorrow, we will continue this fight, and I will not show you mercy as I have done today.'

'I will come tomorrow,' said Ranji. 'I will be ready for you.'

They turned from each other then, and going to their respective rocks put on their clothes, and left the forest by different routes.

When Ranji got home, he found it difficult to explain his cuts and bruises that showed on his face, legs and arms. It was difficult to conceal the fact that he had been in an unusually violent fight, and his mother insisted on his staying at home for the rest of the day. That evening, though, he slipped out of the house and went to the bazaar, where he found comfort and solace in a bottle of vividly coloured lemonade and a banana-leaf full of hot, sweet *jalebis*. He had just finished the lemonade when he saw his adversary coming down the road. His first impulse was to turn away and look elsewhere; his second to throw the lemonade bottle at his enemy; but he did neither of these things. Instead, he stood his ground and scowled at his passing adversary. And the Punjabi boy said nothing either, but scowled back with equal ferocity.

The next day was as hot as the previous one. Ranji felt weak and lazy and not at all eager for a fight. His body was stiff and sore after the previous day's encounter. But he could not refuse the challenge. Not to turn up at the pool would be an acknowledgement of defeat. From the way he felt just then, he knew he would be beaten in another fight; but he could not acquiesce in his own defeat; he must defy his enemy to the last, or outwit him, for only then could he gain his respect. If he surrendered now, he would be beaten for all time; but to fight and be beaten today left him free to fight and be beaten again. As long as he fought, he had a right to the pool in the forest.

He was half hoping that the Punjabi boy would have forgotten the challenge; but these hopes were dashed when he saw his opponent sitting, stripped to the waist, on a rock on the other side of the pool. The Punjabi boy was rubbing oil on his body, massaging it into his broad thighs. He saw Ranji beneath the *sal* trees, and called a challenge across the waters of the pool.

'Come over on this side, and fight!' he shouted.

But Ranji was not going to submit to any conditions laid down by his opponent.

'Come *this* side and fight!' he shouted back with equal vigour.

'Swim across, and fight me here!' called the other. 'Or perhaps you cannot swim the length of this pool?'

But Ranji could have swum the length of the pool a dozen times without tiring, and here he would show the Punjabi boy his superiority. So, slipping out of his vest and shorts, he dived

83

straight into the water, cutting through it like a knife, and surfacing with hardly a splash. The Punjabi boy's mouth hung open in amazement.

'You can dive!' he exclaimed.

'It is easy,' said Ranji, treading water, waiting for a further challenge. 'Can't you dive?'

'No,' said the other. 'I jump straight in. But if you will tell me how, I will make a dive.'

'It is easy,' said Ranji. 'Stand on the rock, stretch your arms out and allow your head to displace your feet.'

*

The Punjabi boy stood up, stiff and straight, stretched out his arms, and threw himself into the water. He landed flat on his belly, with a crash that sent the birds screaming out of the trees.

Ranji dissolved into laughter.

'Are you trying to empty the pool?' he asked, as the Punjabi boy came to the surface, spouting water like a small whale.

'Wasn't it good?' asked the boy, evidently proud of his feat.

'Not very good,' said Ranji. 'You should have more practice. See, I will do it again.'

And pulling himself up on a rock, he executed another perfect dive. The other boy waited for him to come up, but, swimming under water, Ranji circled him and came upon him from behind.

'How did you do that?' asked the astonished youth.

'Can't you swim under water?' asked Ranji.

'No, but I will try it.'

The Punjabi boy made a tremendous effort to plunge to the bottom of the pool; and indeed, he thought he had gone right down, though his bottom, like a duck's, remained above the surface.

Ranji, however, did not discourage him.

'It was not bad,' he said. 'But you need a lot of practice.'

'Will you teach me?' asked his enemy.

'If you like, I will teach you.'

'You must teach me. If you do not teach me, I will beat you. Will you come here every day and teach me?'

'If you like,' said Ranji. They had pulled themselves out of the water, and were sitting side by side on a smooth grey rock.

84

'My name is Suraj,' said the Punjabi boy. 'What is yours?'

'It is Ranji.'

'I am strong, am I not?' said Suraj, bending his arm so that a ball of muscle stood up stretching the white of his flesh.

'You are strong,' said Ranji. 'You are a real *pahelwan.*'

'One day I will be the world's champion wrestler,' said Suraj, slapping his thighs, which shook with the impact of his hand. He looked critically at Ranji's hard, thin body. 'You are quite strong yourself,' he conceded. 'But you are too bony. I know, you people do not eat enough. You must come and have your food with me. I drink one seer of milk every day. We have got our own cow! Be my friend, and I will make you a *pahelwan* like me! I know—if you teach me to dive and swim under water, I will make you a *pahelwan!* That is fair, isn't it?'

'That is fair!' said Ranji, though he doubted if he was getting the better of the exchange.

Suraj put his arm around the younger boy, and said, 'We are friends now, yes?'

They looked at each other with honest, unflinching eyes, and in that moment love and understanding were born.

'We are friends,' said Ranji.

The birds had settled again in their branches, and the pool was quiet and limpid in the shade of the *sal* trees.

'It is our pool,' said Suraj. 'Nobody else can come here without our permission. Who would dare?'

'Who would dare?' said Ranji, smiling with the knowledge that he had won the day.

The Tunnel

It was almost noon, and the jungle was very still, very silent. Heat waves shimmered along the railway embankment where it cut a path through the tall evergreen trees. The railway lines were two straight black serpents disappearing into the tunnel in the hillside.

Ranji stood near the cutting, waiting for the mid-day train. It wasn't a station and he wasn't catching a train. He was waiting so he could watch the steam-engine come roaring out of the tunnel.

He had cycled out of town and taken the jungle path until he had come to a small village. He had left the cycle there, and walked over a low, scrub covered hill and down to the tunnel exit.

Now he looked up. He had heard, in the distance, the shrill whistle of the engine. He couldn't see anything, because the train was approaching from the other side of the hill; but presently a sound like distant thunder came from the tunnel, and he knew the train was coming through.

A second or two later the steam-engine shot out of the tunnel, snorting and puffing like some green, black and gold dragon, some beautiful monster out of Ranji's dreams. Showering sparks right and left, it roared a challenge to the jungle.

Instinctively Ranji stepped back a few paces. Waves of hot steam struck him in the face. Even the trees seemed to flinch from the noise and heat. And then the train had gone, leaving only a plume of smoke to drift lazily over the tall *shisham* trees.

The jungle was still again. No one moved.

Ranji turned from watching the drifting smoke and began walking along the embankment towards the tunnel. It grew darker the further he walked, and when he had gone about twenty yards it became pitch black. He had to turn and look back at the opening to make sure that there was a speck of daylight in the distance.

Ahead of him, the tunnel's other opening was also a small round circle of light.

The walls of the tunnel were damp and sticky. A bat flew past. A lizard scuttled between the lines. Coming straight from the darkness into the light, Ranji was dazzled by the sudden glare. He put a hand up to shade his eyes and looked up at the scrub-covered hillside, and he thought he saw something moving between the trees.

It was just a flash of gold and black, and a long swishing tail. It was there between the trees for a second or two, and then it was gone.

*

About fifty feet from the entrance to the tunnel stood the watchman's hut. Marigolds grew in front of the hut, and at the back there was a small vegetable patch. It was the watchman's duty to inspect the tunnel and keep it clear of obstacles.

Every day, before the train came through, he would walk the length of the tunnel. If all was well, he would return to his hut and take a nap. If something was wrong, he would walk back up the line and wave a red flag and the engine-driver would slow down.

At night, the watchman lit an oil-lamp and made a similar inspection. If there was any danger to the train, he'd go back up the line and wave his lamp to the approaching engine. If all was well, he'd hang his lamp at the door of his hut and go to sleep.

He was just settling down on his cot for an afternoon nap when he saw the boy come out of the tunnel. He waited until the boy was only a few feet away and then said, 'Welcome, welcome. I don't often get visitors. Sit down for a while, and tell me why you were inspecting my tunnel.'

'Is it your tunnel?' asked Ranji.

'It is,' said the watchman. 'It is truly my tunnel, since no one else will have anything to do with it. I have only lent it to the Government.'

Ranji sat down on the edge of the cot.

'I wanted to see the train come through,' he said. 'And then, when it had gone, I decided to walk through the tunnel.'

'And what did you find in it?'

'Nothing. It was very dark. But when I came out, I thought I saw an animal—up on the hill—but I'm not sure, it moved off very quickly.'

'It was a leopard you saw,' said the watchman. 'My leopard.'

'Do you own a leopard too?'

'I do.'

'And do you lend it to the Government?'

'I do not.'

'Is it dangerous?'

'Not if you leave it alone. It comes this way for a few days every month, because there are still deer in this jungle, and the deer is its natural prey. It keeps away from people.'

'Have you been here a long time?' asked Ranji.

'Many years. My name is Kishan Singh.'

'Mine is Ranji.'

'There is one train during the day. And there is one train during the night. Have you seen the Night Mail come through the tunnel?'

'No. At what time does it come?'

'About nine o'clock, if it isn't late. You could come and sit here with me, if you like. And after it has gone, I will take you home.'

'I'll ask my parents.' said Ranji. 'Will it be safe?'

'It is safer in the jungle than in the town. No rascals out here. Only last week, when I went into the town, I had my pocket picked! Leopards don't pick pockets.'

Kishan Singh stretched himself out on his cot. 'And now I am going to take a nap, my friend. It is too hot to be up and about in the afternoon.'

'Everyone goes to sleep in the afternoon,' complained Ranji. 'My father lies down as soon as he's had his lunch.'

'Well, the animals also rest in the heat of the day. It is only the tribe of boys who cannot, or will not, rest.'

Kishan Singh placed a large banana-leaf over his face to keep away the flies, and was soon snoring gently. Ranji stood up, looking up and down the railway tracks. Then he began walking back to the village.

*

The following evening, towards dusk, as the flying-foxes swooped silently out of the trees, Ranji made his way to the watchman's hut.

It had been a long hot day, but now the earth was cooling and a light breeze was moving through the trees. It carried with it the scent of mango blossom, the promise of rain.

Kishan Singh was waiting for Ranji. He had watered his small garden and the flowers looked cool and fresh. A kettle was boiling on an oil-stove.

'I am making tea,' he said. 'There is nothing like a glass of hot sweet tea while waiting for a train.'

They drank their tea, listening to the sharp notes of the tailor-bird and the noisy chatter of the seven-sisters. As the brief twilight faded, most of the birds fell silent. Kishan lit his oil-lamp and said it was time for him to inspect the tunnel. He moved off towards the dark entrance, while Ranji sat on the cot, sipping tea.

In the dark, the trees seemed to move closer. And the night life of the forest was conveyed on the breeze—the sharp call of a barking-deer, the cry of a fox, the quaint tonk-tonk of a nightjar.

There were some sounds that Ranji would not recognize—sounds that came from the trees, creakings, and whisperings, as though the trees were coming alive, stretching their limbs in the dark, shifting a little, flexing their fingers.

Kishan Singh stood outside the tunnel, trimming his lamp. The night sounds were familiar to him and he did not give them much thought; but something else—a padded footfall, a rustle of dry leaves—made him stand still for a few seconds, peering into the darkness. Then, humming softly, he returned to where Ranji was waiting. Then minutes remained for the Night Mail to arrive.

As the watchman sat down on the cot beside Ranji, a new sound reached both of them quite distinctly—a rhythmic sawing sound, as of someone cutting through the branch of a tree.

'What's that?' whispered Ranji.

'It's the leopard,' said Kishan Singh. 'I think it's in the tunnel.'

'The train will soon be here.'

'Yes, my friend. And if we don't drive the leopard out of the tunnel, it will be run over by the engine.'

'But won't it attack us if we try to drive it out?' asked Ranji, beginning to share the watchman's concern.

'It knows me well. We have seen each other many times. I don't think it will attack. Even so, I will take my axe along. You had better stay here, Ranji.'

'No, I'll come too. It will be better than sitting here alone in the dark.'

'All right, but stay close behind me. And remember, there is nothing to fear.'

Raising his lamp, Kishan Singh walked into the tunnel, shouting at the top of his voice to try and scare away the animal. Ranji followed close behind. But he found he was unable to do any shouting; his throat had gone quite dry.

They had gone about twenty paces into the tunnel when the light from the lamp fell upon the leopard. It was crouching between the tracks, only fifteen feet away from them. Baring its teeth and snarling, it went down on its belly, tail twitching. Ranji felt sure it was going to spring at them.

Kishan Singh and Ranji both shouted together. Their voices rang through the tunnel. And the leopard, uncertain as to how many terrifying humans were there in front of him, turned swiftly and disappeared into the darkness.

To make sure it had gone, Ranji and the watchman walked the length of the tunnel. When they returned to the entrance, the rails were beginning to hum. They knew the train was coming.

Ranji put his hand to one of the rails and felt its tremor. He heard the distant rumble of the train. And then the engine came round the bend, hissing at them, scattering sparks into the darkness, defying the jungle as it roared through the steep sides of the cutting. It charged straight into the tunnel, thundering past Ranji like the beautiful dragon of his dreams.

And when it had gone, the silence returned and the forest seemed to breathe, to live again. Only the rails still trembled with the passing of the train.

*

They trembled again to the passing of the same train, almost a week later, when Ranji and his father were both travelling in it.

Ranji's father was scribbling in a notebook, doing his accounts. How boring of him, thought Ranji as he sat near an open window staring out at the darkness. His father was going to Delhi on a business trip and had decided to take the boy along.

'It's time you learnt something about the business,' he had said, to Ranji's dismay.

The Night Mail rushed through the forest with its hundreds of passengers. The carriage wheels beat out a steady rhythm on the rails. Tiny flickering lights came and went, as they passed small villages on the fringe of the jungle.

Ranji heard the rumble as the train passed over a small bridge. It was too dark to see the hut near the cutting, but he knew they must be approaching the tunnel. He strained his eyes looking out into the night; and then, just as the engine let out a shrill whistle, Ranji saw the lamp.

He couldn't see Kishan Singh, but he saw the lamp, and he knew that his friend was out there.

The train went into the tunnel and out again, it left the jungle behind and thundered across the endless plains. And Ranji stared out at the darkness, thinking of the lonely cutting in the forest, and the watchman with the lamp who would always remain a fire-fly for those travelling thousands, as he lit up the darkness for steam-engines and leopards.

The Summer Season

It was in the spring that Visni presented himself at the Roxy cinema and asked for a job. He was fourteen. He had the light, soft-brown skin of the hill people, with black eyes and dark unruly hair. He had walked into the hill-station from his village, which lay over thirty miles away, behind two ranges of mountains. After his father's death it had been decided that Visni should go into the town to find work, while his mother, sister, and two small brothers looked after their fields in Garhwal, scraping a scant living from the rocky soil.

The Roxy was the hill-station's only cinema, and remained open for six months in the year, from April to October. During this period it did good business, for the town was crowded with tourists and holiday-makers who had come up from the plains to escape the heat. But during the winter months the town was deserted, the shops and restaurants would be closed, and if one walked a little way out of the town one was more likely to meet a bear than a human being.

When Visni came into town, after a day and a half's walking, he was wearing a thin cotton shirt, short pants, and an old pair of tennis shoes. The days were warm and sunny, and this clothing was sufficient. In the bag he carried with him was a blanket, and in his shirt pocket he had six rupees, and that was all.

At first he had tried to get work in a tea-shop, but they didn't need any more helpers. On his second day in town, after spending the night in a shed meant for rickshaw-pullers, he went to the cinema, where the proprietor of the cinema's tea-stall engaged him. The proprietor was in need of a new boy, having just sacked the previous one for his general clumsiness. Visni's job was to help prepare tea and *samosas* serve refreshments to the public during intervals in the film, and later wash up the plates and cups. His pay would be thirty rupees a month—including as much free tea as he could drink....

Visni went to work immediately, and it was not long before he was as well-versed in his duties as the other two tea-boys, Chitru and Ram Parshad. Chitru was a lazy good-for-nothing who always tried to place the brunt of his work on someone else's shoulders; but he was generous, and had lent Visni five rupees during the first week. Ram Parshad, besides being a tea-boy, had the enviable job of being the poster-boy as well. (He was paid extra for this.) As the cinema was closed till three in the afternoon, Ram Parshad was engaged either in pushing the big poster-board around the town, or sticking posters on convenient walls. 'It keeps the walls from falling down,' he said. This suited him nicely, as he could go where he liked, visit friends, and stop in at restaurants for a smoke, a chat or a light meal.

Chitru had relatives in town and slept at their house. Both Visni and Ram Parshad were on their own, and had to sleep at the cinema. They were not provided with any accommodation. The hall was closed at night, after the last show, so it was not possible for them to settle down comfortably in the expensive seats, as they would have liked; they had to sleep in the open foyer, near the ticket office, where they were often at the mercy of icy Himalayan winds.

But Ram Parshad made things comfortable by setting his poster-board at an angle to the wall, which gave them a small alcove where they could sleep protected from the wind. As Visni and Ram Parshad had only one blanket each, and the nights were cold, they placed their blankets together and rolled themselves into a warm, round ball. Ram Parshad smoked innumerable *bidis*, and his breath, which held the aroma, was at first disconcerting to Visni; but Visni soon got used to this, as he got used to Ram Parshad's many unhygienic habits, like bathing only once a month and using his finger to clean his teeth about once a week.

Every morning Visni scrubbed his teeth with a twig of *neem*, and soaped himself well at the public tap. Ram Parshad was pleased by the freshness of Visni's body, and enjoyed watching him bathe, and sometimes even condescended to rub his friend's body with mustard oil; but he was supremely indifferent to his own body—perhaps the dirt he accumulated on it kept him warm on cold nights. That, at any rate, was the explanation he gave for his slovenliness....Despite all this, Visni could not help liking Ram Parshad, for his good humour, unselfish nature, and even a little for his untidiness which made him attractive in an unattractive way.

The new pictures started their run on a Friday, and over the week-end large crowds would gather at the cinema, clamouring for tickets. There was quite a black market in tickets, as the first comers would buy up about two dozen and then sell them at higher prices to people who stood little chance of getting in. This would anger others in the crowd; people would start shouting and pushing and climbing over one another's heads. Sometimes there would be a free-for-all, and if a lone policeman attempted to bring about order he might find himself at the bottom of a heap of struggling bodies. Visni was alarmed when he first saw this happen, but Ram Parshad assured him that it took place regularly every week-end, and that none of the hostility was directed at the boys. But in the hall itself, when Visni brought the tea around, some of the people (not confined to the cheaper seats) would be rude and disagreeable. When Visni spilt some tea over an aggressive college student's shoes, he received a vicious kick on the shin. He complained to the tea-stall proprietor; but his employer said, 'The customer is always right. You should have got out of the way in time!'

As he began to get used to the life and to the tempo of his work, Visni found himself taking an interest in his patrons. He feared the occupants of the cheaper seats, whose language was often free and uninhibited; he was timid and shy of the people in the balcony, and usually left them to Chitru; but he felt quite happy with the people in between, those who were neither very crude nor very sophisticated, though they certainly had peculiarities of their own.

There was, for instance, the large gentleman with the soup-strainer moustache, who drank his tea from the saucer. When he drank, his lips worked on the principle of a suction pump, and the tea, after some brief agitation in the saucer, would disappear in a matter of seconds. Visni often wondered if there was something lurking in the forests of that gentleman's upper lip, something that would suddenly spring out and fall upon him! The boys took great pleasure in exchanging anecdotes about the eccentricities of some customers.

Visni had never seen such bright, painted women before. The girls in his village had been healthy and good-looking; but they did not smell and talk as mysteriously as these women who had come up from the plains for the summer season. Dressed in fine clothes, painted and perfumed, they chattered about inconsequentials of vast importance, and never gave Visni more than a brief, bored glance. Middle-aged women were more inclined to notice him, and favoured him with kind words and sometimes a small tip when he took away the cups. He found he could make a rupee or two every week in tips; and when he received his first month's pay, he sent half of it home.

*

Visni never had a holiday, but in the mornings he was free, and then he would join other boys in flying kites from the top of the hill, or he would play football on the *maidan*. Football was great fun, especially during the monsoon rains, when the field became a bog, the football slippery and elusive. Then there was *kabbadi*, a vigorous game that called for strong legs and healthy lungs; and occasional dips in the cool stream that tumbled down the mountain into the valley. Whenever one of Visni's playmates came to a picture, Visni would slip him a free cup of tea.

Soon he had an extensive knowledge of films and film-stars, and knew the lyrics of all the popular songs. Once he even managed to pinch a couple of photo-stills, and sold them to a well-to-do young student for five rupees.

And so, throughout the summer, life carried on more or less on the same even keel.

As the night show finished at about twelve, Visni would wake late in the morning. He would eat with Ram Parshad, cooking his own food, sharing the expenses. This was their only big meal; the rest was made up of snacks during the film-time, and innumerable cups of tea. The cinema did well throughout the summer, but when the monsoon rains set in, the town began to empty. A thick mist lay over the town for days on end. When the rains passed, and the mists cleared, an autumn wind came whispering through the pine trees. Visni couldn't sleep so well, as the cold crept through the blankets and into his bones.

At the end of September the manager of the Roxy gave everyone a week's notice, a week's pay, and announced that the cinema was closing for winter months.

Ram Parshad said, 'I'm going down to the plains to find work. I shall come back next year. What about you, Visni, why don't you come with me? It's easier to find work in the plains.'

'I'm going home,' said Visni. 'I don't know if I'll come back next season. I have land of my own. I think it is better to work on my own land, even if it is more difficult.'

'I like the towns,' said Ram Parshad. 'I like the shops and people and lots of noise. I will never go back to my village again. There is no money to be made there.'

Ram Parshad made a bundle of his things and set out on foot for the railway terminus at the bottom of the hill. Chitru went to his relatives, to hibernate until the spring came. Visni rolled up his blanket, and with the money he had saved, bought himself a pair of *chappals*; his old shoes had worn away, compelling him to go barefoot for a month.

*

It snowed during his last night in town. He slept alone behind the poster-board, for Ram Parshad had gone. The wind blew the snow-flakes into the open foyer, and went whistling down the still, deserted streets. In the morning Visni opened his eyes on a world of dazzling white. The snow was piled high against the poster-board, obscuring most of the glamorous film actress who smiled emptily at the unresponsive mountains.

Visni went to a tea-shop, drank a glass of hot sweet tea, and ate two buns. Then he set out on his march home.

As his village lay further to the north, he went deeper into the snow. His feet were blue with the cold, and after some time he wasn't conscious of having any feet at all. He trudged through the forests all day, stopping only at villages to take refreshment. By nightfall he was still ten miles from home. But he had fallen in with other travellers, mule-drivers mostly, and with them he found shelter in a small village. They built a fire and crowded round it, and each man spoke of his home, and someone sang, and someone told a story of evil spirits and mysterious disappearances—happenings that were peculiar to that area. Visni felt at home with these strong, simple men, and fell asleep listening to their tales. In the morning they parted and went different ways.

It was almost noon when Visni reached his village. The fields were covered with snow, and the mountain stream that passed through the village was in full spate. As he climbed the hill to his house—it was the highest house in the village—he heard the sound of barking, and his mother's big black Bhotia dog came bounding towards him over the snow. The dog jumped on him and licked his face, and then went bounding back to the house to tell the others.

Visni's smallest brother saw him next, and turned and ran indoors, shouting, 'Visni has come! Visni has come!'

The other brother ran out of the house, shouting, 'Visni, Visni!'

Visni came walking through the fields, and he didn't hurry, he didn't run, though he saw his mother and sister standing in front of the house, waiting for him. There was no need to hurry now. He would be with them for a long time, and the manager of the Roxy would have to find someone else for the next summer season. . . . .It was his house, and they were his fields; even the snow was his. When the snow melted he would clear these fields, and nourish them, and make them rich.

He felt very big and very strong as he came striding over the land he loved.

Going Home

The train came panting through the forest and into the flat brown plain. The engine whistled piercingly, and a few cows moved off the track. In a swaying third-class compartment two men played cards; a women held a baby to an exposed breast; a Sikh labourer, wearing brief pants, lay asleep on an upper bunk, snoring fitfully; an elderly unshaven man chewed the last of his *pan* and spat the red juice out of the window. A small boy, mischief in his eyes, jingled a bag of coins in front of an anxious farmer.

Daya Ram, the farmer, was going home; home to his rice fields, his buffalo and his wife. A brother had died recently, and Daya Ram had taken the ashes to Hardwar to immerse them in the holy waters of the Ganga, and now he was on the train to Dehra and soon he would be home. He was looking anxious because he had just remembered his wife's admonition about being careful with money; ten rupees was what he had left with him, and it was all in the bag the boy held.

'Let me have it now,' said Daya Ram, 'before the money falls out.' He made a grab at the little bag that contained his coins, notes and railway ticket, but the boy shrieked with delight and leapt out of the way.

Daya Ram stroked his moustache; it was a long drooping moustache that lent a certain sadness to his somewhat kind and foolish face. He reflected that it was his own fault for having started the game; the child had been sulky and morose, and, to cheer him up, Daya Ram had begun jingling his money. Now the boy was jingling the money, right in front of the open window.

'Come now, give it back,' pleaded Daya Ram, 'or I shall tell your mother.'

The boy's mother had her back to them, and it was a large back, almost as forbidding as her front. But the boy was enjoying his game and would not give up the bag; he was exploiting to the full Daya Ram's easy-going tolerant nature, and kept bobbing up and down on the seat, waving the bag in the poor man's face.

Suddenly the boy's mother, who had been engrossed in conversation with another woman, turned and saw what was happening. She walloped the boy over the head and the suddenness of the blow (it was more of a thump than a slap) made him fall back against the window, and the cloth bag fell from his hand on to the railway embankment outside.

Now Daya Ram's first impulse was to leap out of the moving train. But when someone shouted, 'Pull the alarm cord!' he decided on this course of action. He plunged for the alarm cord, but just at that moment someone else shouted, 'Don't pull the cord!' and Daya Ram who usually listened to others, stood in suspended animation, waiting for further directions.

'Too many people are stopping trains every day all over India,' said one of the card players, who wore large thick-rimmed spectacles over a pair of tiny humourless eyes, and was obviously a post office counter-clerk. 'You people are becoming a menace to the railways.'

'Exactly,' said the other card-player. 'You stop the train on the most trifling excuses. What is your trouble?'

'My money has fallen out.' said Daya Ram.

'Why didn't you say so!' exclaimed the clerk, jumping up. 'Stop the train!'

'Sit down,' said his companion, 'its too late now. The train cannot wait here until he walks half a mile back down the line. How much did you lose?' he asked Daya Ram.

'Ten rupees.'

'And you have no more?'

Daya Ram shook his head.

'Then you had better leave the train at the next station and go back for it.'

The next station, Harrawala, was about ten miles from the spot where the money had fallen. Daya Ram got down from the train and started back along the railway track. He was a well-built man, with strong legs and a dark, burnished skin. He wore a vest and *dhoti*, and had a red cloth tied round his head. He walked with long, easy steps, but the ground had been scorched by the burning sun, and it was not long before his feet were smarting; his eyes too were unaccustomed to the glare of the plains, and he held a hand up over them, or looked at the ground. The sun was high in the sky, beating down on his bare arms and legs. Soon his body was running with sweat, his vest was soaked through and sticking to his skin.

There were no trees anywhere near the lines, which ran straight to the hazy blue horizon. There were fields in the distance, and cows grazed on short grass, but there were no humans in sight. After an hour's walk, Daya Ram felt thirsty; his tongue was furred, his gums dry, his lips like parchment. When he saw a buffalo wallowing in a muddy pool, he hurried to the spot and drank thirstily of the stagnant water.

Still, his pace did not slacken. He knew of only one way to walk, and that was at his steady long pace. At the end of another hour he felt sure he had passed the place where the bag had fallen. He had been inspecting the embankment very closely, and now he felt discouraged and dispirited. But still he walked on. He was worried more by the thought of his wife's attitude than by the loss of the money or the problem of the next meal.

*

Rather than turn back, he continued walking until he reached the next station. He kept following the lines, and after half an hour dragged his aching feet on to Raiwala platform. To his surprise and joy, he saw a note in Hindi on the notice board: 'Anyone having lost a bag containing some notes and coins may enquire at the station-master's office.' Some honest man or woman or child had found the bag and handed it in. Daya Ram felt that his faith in the goodness of human nature had been justified.

He rushed into the office and, pushing aside an indignant clerk, exclaimed: 'You have found my money!'

'What money?' snapped the harassed-looking official. 'And don't just charge in here shouting at the top of your voice; this is not a hotel!'

'The money I lost on the train,' said Daya Ram. 'Ten rupees.'

'In notes or in coins?' asked the station-master, who was not slow in assessing a situation.

'Six one-rupee notes,' said Daya Ram. 'The rest in coins.'

100

'Hmmm. . . .and what was the purse like?'

'White cloth,' said Daya Ram. 'Dirty white cloth,' he added for clarification.

The official put his hand in a drawer, took out the bag and flung it across the desk. Without further parley, Daya Ram scooped up the bag and burst through the swing doors, completely revived after his fatiguing march.

*

Now he had only one idea: to celebrate, in his small way, the recovery of his money.

So, he left the station and made his way through a sleepy little bazaar to the nearest tea shop. He sat down at a table and asked for tea and a hookah. The shopkeeper placed a record on a gramophone, and the shrill music shattered the afternoon silence of the bazaar.

A young man sitting idly at the next table smiled at Daya Ram and said, 'You are looking happy, brother.'

Daya Ram beamed. 'I lost my money and found it,' he said simply.

'Then you should celebrate with something stronger than tea,' said the friendly stranger with a wink. 'Come on into the next room.' He took Daya Ram by the arm and was so comradely that the older man felt pleased and flattered. They went behind a screen, and then the shopkeeper brought them two glasses and a bottle of country-made rum.

Before long, Daya Ram had told his companion the story of his life. He had also paid for the rum and was prepared to pay for more. But two of the young man's friends came in and suggested a card-game, and Daya Ram, who remembered having once played a game of cards in his youth, showed enthusiasm. He lost sportingly, to the tune of five rupees; the rum had such a benevolent effect on his already genial nature that he was quite ready to go on playing until he had lost everything, but the shopkeeper came in hurriedly with the information that a policeman was hanging about outside. Daya Ram's table companions promptly disappeared.

Daya Ram was still happy. He paid for the hookah and the cup of tea he hadn't had, and went lurching into the street. He had some vague intention of returning to the station to catch a train, and had his ticket in his hand; by now his sense of direction was so confused that he turned down a side-alley and was soon lost in a labyrinth of tiny alley-ways. Just when he thought he saw trees ahead, his attention was drawn to a man leaning against a wall and groaning wretchedly. The man was in rags, his hair was tousled, and his face looked bruised.

*

Daya Ram heard his groans and stumbled over to him.

'What is wrong?' he asked with concern. 'What is the matter with you?'

'I have been robbed,' said the man, speaking with difficulty. 'Two thugs beat me and took my money. Don't go any further this way.'

'Can I do anything for you?' said Daya Ram. 'Where do you live?'

'No, I will be all right,' said the man, leaning heavily on Daya Ram. 'Just help me to the corner of the road, and then I can find my way.'

'Do you need anything?' said Daya Ram. 'Do you need any money?'

'No, no just help me to those steps.'

Daya Ram put an arm around the man and helped him across the road, seating him on a step.

'Are you sure I can do nothing for you?' persisted Daya Ram.

The man shook his head and closed his eyes, leaning back against the wall. Daya Ram hesitated a little, and then left. But as soon as Daya Ram turned the corner, the man opened his eyes. He transferred the bag of money from the fold of his shirt to the string of his pyjamas. Then, completely recovered, he was up and away.

Daya Ram discovered his loss when he had gone about fifty yards, and then it was too late. He was puzzled, but was not upset. So many things happened to him today, and he was confused and unaware of his real situation. He still had his ticket, and that was what mattered most.

The train was at the station, and Daya Ram got into a half-empty compartment. It was only when the train began to move that he came to his senses and realized what had befallen him. As the engine gathered speed, his thoughts came faster. He was not worried (except by the thought of his wife) and he was not unhappy, but he was puzzled; he was not angry or resentful, but he was a little hurt. He knew he had been tricked, but he couldn't understand why; he had really liked those people he had met in the tea shop of Raiwala, and he still could not bring himself to believe that the man in rags had been putting on an act.

'Have you got a *bidi*?' asked a man beside him, who looked like another farmer.

Daya Ram had a *bidi*. He gave it to the other man and lit it for him. Soon they were talking about crops and rainfall and their respective families, and although a faint uneasiness still hovered at the back of his mind, Daya Ram had almost forgotten the day's misfortunes. He had his ticket to Dehra and from there he had to walk only three miles, and then he would be home, and there would be hot milk and cooked vegetables waiting for him. He and other farmer chattered away, as the train went panting across the wide brown plain.

Masterji

I was strolling along the platform, waiting for the arrival of the Amritsar Express, when I saw Mr Khushal, handcuffed to a policeman.

I hadn't recognized him at first—a paunchy gentleman with a lot of grey in his beard and a certain arrogant amusement in his manner. It was only when I came closer, and we were almost face to face, that I recognized my old Hindi teacher.

Startled, I stopped and stared. And he stared back at me, a glimmer of recognition in his eyes. It was over twenty years since I'd last seen him, standing jauntily before the classroom blackboard, and now here he was tethered to a policeman and looking as jaunty as ever. . . .

'Good—good evening, Sir', I stammered, in my best public-school manner. (You must always respect your teacher, no matter what the circumstances.)

Mr Kushal's face lit up with pleasure. 'So you remember me! It's nice to see you again, my boy.'

Forgetting that his right hand was shackled to the policeman's left, I made as if to shake hands. Mr Khushal thoughtfully took my right hand in his left and gave it a rough squeeze. A faint odour of cloves and cinnamon reached me, and I remembered how he had always been redolent of spices when standing beside my desk, watching me agonize over my Hindi-English translation.

He had joined the school in 1948, not long after the Partition. Until then there had been no Hindi teacher; we'd been taught Urdu and French. Then came a ruling that Hindi was to be a compulsory subject, and at the age of sixteen I found myself struggling with a new script. When Mr Khushal joined the staff (on the recommendation of a local official), there was no one else in the school who knew Hindi, or who could assess Mr Khushal's abilities as a teacher. . . .

And now once again he stood before me, only this time he was in the custody of the law.

I was still recovering from the shock when the train drew in, and everyone on the platform began making a rush for the compartment doors. As the policeman elbowed his way through the crowd, I kept close behind him and his charge, and as a result I managed to get into the same third-class compartment. I found a seat right opposite Mr Khushal. He did not seem to be the least bit embarrassed by the handcuffs, or by the stares of his fellow-passengers. Rather, it was the policeman who looked unhappy and ill-at-ease.

As the train got under way, I offered Mr Khushal one of the *parathas* made for me by my Ferozepur landlady. He accepted it with alacrity. I offered one to the constable as well, but although he looked at it with undisguised longing, he felt duty-bound to decline.

'Why have they arrested you sir?' I asked. 'Is it very serious?'

'A trivial matter,' said Mr Khushal. 'Nothing to worry about. I shall be at liberty soon.'

'But what did you *do*?'

Mr Khushal leant forward. 'Nothing to be ashamed of,' he said in a confiding tone. 'Even a great teacher like Socrates fell foul of the law.'

'You mean—one of your pupil's—made a complaint?'

'And why should one of my pupils make a complaint?' Mr Khushal looked offended. 'They were the beneficiaries—it was for *them*.' He noticed that I looked mystified, and decided to come straight to the point: 'It was simply a question of false certificates.'

'Oh,' I said, feeling deflated. Public school boys are always prone to jump to the wrong conclusions. . . .

'*Your* certificates, sir?'

'Of course not. Nothing wrong with my certificates—I had them printed in Lahore, in 1946.'

'With age comes respectability,' I remarked. 'In that case, whose. . . .?'

'Why, the matriculation certificates I've been providing all these years to the poor idiots who would never have got through on their own!'

'You mean you gave them you own certificates?'

105

'That's right. And if it hadn't been for so many printing mistakes, no one would have been any wiser. You can't find a good press these days, that's the trouble. . . .It was a public service, my boy, I hope you appreciate that. . . .It isn't fair to hold a boy back in life simply because he can't get through some puny exam. . . .Mind you, I don't give my certificates to *anyone*. They come to me only after they have failed two or three times.'

'And I suppose you charge something?'

'Only if they can pay. There's no fixed sum. Whatever they like to give me. I've never been greedy in these matters, and you know I am not unkind. . . .'

Which is true enough, I thought, looking out of the carriage window at the green fields of Moga and remembering the half-yearly Hindi exam, when I had stared blankly at the question paper, knowing that I was totally incapable of answering any of it. Mr Khushal had come walking down the line of desks stopping at mine and breathing cloves all over me, 'Come on, boy, why haven't you started?'

'Can't do it sir,' I'd said. 'It's too difficult.'

'Never mind,' he'd urged in a whisper. 'Do *something*. Copy it out, copy it out!'

And so, to pass the time, I'd copied out the entire paper, word for word. And a fortnight later, when the results were out, I found I had passed!

'But sir,' I had stammered, approaching Mr Khushal when I found him alone. 'I never answered the paper. I couldn't translate the passage. All I did was copy it out!'

'That's why I gave you pass-marks,' he'd answered imperturbably. 'You have such neat handwriting. If ever you *do* learn Hindi, my boy, you'll write a beautiful script!'

And remembering that moment, I was now filled with compassion for my old teacher; and leaning across, I placed my hand on his knee and said: 'Sir, if they convict you, I hope it won't be for long. And when you come out, if you happen to be in Delhi or Ferozepur, please look me up. You see, I'm still rather hopeless at Hindi, and perhaps you could give me tuition. I'd be glad to pay. . . .'

Mr Khushal threw back his head and laughed, and the entire compartment shook with his laughter.

'Teach you Hindi!' he cried. 'My dear boy, what gave you the idea that I ever knew any Hindi?'

'But, sir—if not Hindi what were you teaching us all the time at school?'

'Punjabi!' he shouted, and everyone jumped in their seats. 'Pure Punjabi! But how were *you* to know the difference?'

Listen to the Wind

March is probably the most uncomfortable month in the hills. The rain is cold, often accompanied by sleet and hail, and the wind from the north comes tearing down the mountain-passes with tremendous force. Those few people who pass the winter in the hill-station remain close to their fires. If they can't afford fires, they get into bed.

I found old Miss Mackenzie tucked up in bed with three hot-water bottles for company. I took the bedroom's single easy chair, and for some time Miss Mackenzie and I listened to the thunder and watched the play of lightning. The rain made a tremendous noise on the corrugated tin roof, and we had to raise our voices in order to be heard. The hills looked blurred and smudgy when seen through the rain-spattered windows. The wind battered at the doors and rushed round the cottage, determined to make an entry; it slipped down the chimney, but stuck there choking and gurgling and protesting helplessly.

'There's a ghost in your chimney and he can't get out,' I said.

'Then let him stay there,' said Miss Mackenzie.

A vivid flash of lightning lit up the opposite hill showing me for a moment a pile of ruins which I never knew were there.

'You're looking at Burnt Hill,' said Miss Mackenzie. 'It always gets the lightning when there's a storm.'

'Possibly there are iron deposits in the rocks,' I said.

'I wouldn't know. But it's the reason why no one ever lived there for long. Almost every dwelling that was put up was struck by lightning and burnt down.'

'I thought I saw some ruins just now.'

'Nothing but rubble. When they were first settling in the hills they chose that spot. Later they moved to the site where the town now stands. Burnt Hill was left to the deer and the leopards and the monkeys—and to its ghosts, of course. . . .'

'Oh, so it's haunted, too.'

'So they say. On evenings such as these. But you don't believe in ghosts, do you?'

'No. Do you?'

'No. But you'll understand why they say the hill is haunted when you hear its story. Listen.'

I listened, but at first I could hear nothing but the wind and the rain. Then Miss Mackenzie's clear voice rose above the sound of the elements, and I heard her saying:

'. . . .it's really the old story of ill-starred lovers, only it's true. I'd met Robert at his parent's house some weeks before the tragedy took place He was eighteen, tall and fresh-looking, and full of manhood. He'd been born out here, but his parents were hoping to return to England when Robert's father retired. His father was a magistrate, I think—but that hasn't any bearing on the story.

'Their plans didn't work out the way they expected. You see, Robert fell in love. Not with an English girl, mind you, but with a hill girl, the daughter of a landholder from the village behind Burnt Hill. Even today it would be unconventional. Twenty-five years ago, it was almost unheard of! Robert liked walking, and he was hiking through the forest when he saw or rather heard her. It was said later that he fell in love with her voice. She was singing, and the song—low and sweet and strange to his ears—struck him to the heart. When he caught sight of the girl's face, he was not disappointed. She was young and beautiful. She saw him and returned his awestruck gaze with a brief, fleeting smile.

'Robert, in his impetuousness, made enquiries at the village, located the girl's father, and without much ado asked for her hand in marriage. He probably thought that a *sahib* would not be refused such a request. At the same time, it was really quite gallant on his part, because any other young man might simply have ravished the girl in the forest. But Robert was in love, and, therefore, completely irrational in his behaviour.

'Of course the girl's father would have nothing to do with the proposal. He was a Brahmin, and he wasn't going to have the good name of his family ruined by marrying off his only daughter to a foreigner. Robert did not argue with the father; nor did he say anything to his own parents, because he knew their reaction would be one of shock and dismay. They would do everything in their power to put an end to his madness.

'But Robert continued to visit the forest—you see it there, that heavy patch of oak and pine—and he often came across the girl, for she would be gathering fodder or fuel. She did not seem to resent his attentions, and, as Robert knew something of the language, he was soon able to convey his feelings to her. The girl must at first have been rather alarmed, but the boy's sincerity broke down her reserve. After all, she was young too—young enough to fall in love with a devoted swain, without thinking too much of his background. She knew her father would never agree to a marriage—and *he* knew his parents would prevent anything like that happening. So they planned to run away together. Romantic, isn't it? But it did happen. Only they did *not* live happily ever after.'

'Did their parents come after them?'

'No. They had agreed to meet one night in the ruined building on Burnt Hill—the ruin you saw just now; it hasn't changed much, except that there was a bit of roof to it then. They left their homes and made their way to the hill without any difficulty. After meeting, they planned to take the little path that followed the course of a stream until it reached the plains. After that—but who knows what they had planned, what dreams of the future they had conjured up? The storm broke soon after they'd reached the ruins. They took shelter under the dripping ceiling. It was a storm just like this one—a high wind and great torrents of rain and hail, and the lightning flitting about and crashing down almost every minute. They must have been soaked, huddled together in a corner of that crumbling building, when lightning struck. No one knows at what time it happened. But next morning their charred bodies were found on the worn yellow stones of the old building.'

Miss Mackenzie stopped speaking, and I noticed that the thunder had grown distant and the rain had lessened; but the chimney was still coughing and clearing its throat.

'That's true, every word of it,' said Miss Mackenzie. 'But as to Burnt Hill being haunted, that's another matter. I've no experience of ghosts.'

'Anyway, you need a fire to keep them out of the chimney,' I said, getting up to go. I had my raincoat and umbrella, and my own cottage was not far away.

Next morning, when I took the steep path up to Burnt Hill, the sky was clear, and though there was still a stiff wind, it was no longer menacing. An hour's climb brought me to the old ruin—now nothing but a heap of stones, as Miss Mackenzie had said. Part of a wall was left, and the corner of a fireplace. Grass and weeds had grown up through the floor, and primroses and wild saxifrage flowered amongst the rubble.

Where had they sheltered I wondered, as the wind tore at them and fire fell from the sky.

I touched upon the cold stones, half expecting to find in them some traces of the warmth of human contact. I listened, waiting for some ancient echo, some returning wave of sound, that would bring me nearer to the spirits of the dead lovers; but there was only the wind coughing in the lovely pines.

I thought I heard voices in the wind; and perhaps I did. For isn't the wind the voice of the undying dead?

The Haunted Bicycle

I was living at the time in a village about five miles out of Shahganj, a district in east Uttar Pradesh, and my only means of transport was a bicycle. I could of course have gone into Shahganj on any obliging farmer's bullock-cart, but, in spite of bad roads and my own clumsiness as a cyclist, I found the bicycle a trifle faster. I went into Shahganj almost every day, collected my mail, bought a newspaper, drank innumerable cups of tea, and gossiped with the tradesmen. I cycled back to the village at about six in the evening, along a quiet, unfrequented forest road. During the winter months it was dark by six, and I would have to use a lamp on the bicycle.

One evening, when I had covered about half the distance to the village, I was brought to a halt by a small boy who was standing in the middle of the road. The forest at that late hour was no place for a child: wolves and hyaenas were common in the district. I got down from my bicycle and approached the boy, but he didn't seem to take much notice of me.

'What are you doing here on your own?' I asked.

'I'm waiting,' he said, without looking at me.

'Waiting for whom? Your parents?'

'No, I am waiting for my sister.'

'Well, I haven't passed her on the road,' I said. 'She may be further ahead. You had better come along with me, we'll soon find her.'

The boy nodded and climbed silently on to the crossbar in front of me. I have never been able to recall his features. Already it was dark and besides, he kept his face turned away from me.

The wind was against us, and as I cycled on, I shivered with the cold, but the boy did not seem to feel it. We had not gone far when the light from my lamp fell on the figure of another child who was standing by the side of the road. This time it was a girl. She was a little older than the boy, and her hair was long

112

and wind-swept, hiding most of her face.

'Here's your sister,' I said. 'Let's take her along with us.'

The girl did not respond to my smile, and she did no more than nod seriously to the boy; but she climbed up on my back carrier, and allowed me to pedal off again. Their replies to my friendly questions were monosyllabic, and I gathered that they were wary of strangers. Well, when I got to the village, I would hand them over to the headman, and he could locate their parents.

The road was level, but I felt as though I was cycling uphill. And then I noticed that the boy's head was much closer to my face, that the girl's breathing was loud and heavy, almost as though she was doing the riding. Despite the cold wind, I began to feel hot and suffocated.

'I think we'd better take a rest,' I suggested.

'No!' cried the boy and girl together. 'No rest!'

I was so surprised that I rode on without any argument; and then, just as I was thinking of ignoring their demand and stopping, I noticed that the boy's hands, which were resting on the handle-bar, had grown long and black and hairy.

My hands shook and the bicycle wobbled about on the road.

'Be careful!' shouted the children in unison. 'Look where you're going!'

Their tone now was menacing and far from childlike. I took a quick glance over my shoulder and had my worst fears confirmed. The girl's face was huge and bloated. Her legs, black and hairy, were trailing along the ground.

'Stop!' ordered the terrible children. 'Stop near the stream!'

But before I could do anything, my front wheel hit a stone and the bicycle toppled over. As I sprawled in the dust, I felt something hard, like a hoof, hit me on the back of the head, and then there was total darkness.

When I recovered consciousness, I noticed that the moon had risen and was sparkling on the waters of a stream. The children were not to be seen anywhere. I got up from the ground and began to brush the dust from my clothes. And then, hearing the sound of splashing and churning in the stream, I looked up again.

Two small black buffaloes gazed at me from the muddy, moonlit water.

Dead Man's Gift

'A dead man is no good to anyone,' said Nathu the old *shikari*, as he stared into the glowing embers of the camp-fire and wrapped a thin blanket around his thin shoulders.

We had spent a rewarding but tiring day in the Terai forests near Haldwani, where I had been photographing swamp-deer. On our return to the forest rest-house, Nathu had made a log-fire near the front verandah, and we had gathered round it—Nathu, myself and Ghanshyam Singh the *chowkidar*—discussing a suicide that had taken place in a neighbouring village. I forget the details of the suicide—it was connected with a disappointed bridegroom—but the discussion led to some interesting reminiscences on the part of Ghanshyam Singh.

We had all agreed with Nathu's sentiments about dead men, when Ghanshyam interrupted to say, 'I don't know about that, brother. At least one dead man brought considerable good fortune to a friend of mine.'

'How was that?' I asked.

'Well, about twenty years ago,' said Ghanshyam Singh, 'I was a policeman, one of the six constables at a small police post in the village of Ahirpur near the hills. A small stream ran past the village. Fed by springs, it contained a few feet of water even during the hottest of seasons, while after heavy rain it became a roaring torrent. The head constable in charge of our post was Dilawar Singh, who came from a good family which had fallen on evil days. He was a handsome fellow, very well-dressed, always spending his money before he received it. He was passionately fond of good horseflesh, and the mare he rode was a beautiful creature named Leila. He had obtained the mare by paying two hundred and fifty rupees down, and promising to pay the remaining two hundred and fifty in six months time. If he failed to do so, he would have to return the mare and forfeit the deposit. But Dilawar Singh expected to be able to borrow the balance from Lala Ram Das, the wealthy *bania* of Ahirpur.

'The *bania* of Ahirpur was one of the meanest alive. You know the sort, fat and flabby from overeating and sitting all day in his shop, but very wealthy. His house was a large one, situated near the stream, at some distance from the village.'

'But why did he live outside the village, away from his customers?' I asked.

'It made no difference to him,' said Ghanshyam. 'Everyone was in his debt, and, whether they liked it or not, were compelled to deal with him. His father had lived inside the village but had been looted by dacoits, whose ill-treatment had left him a cripple for life. Not a single villager had come to his assistance on that occasion. He had never forgotten it. He built himself another house outside the village, with a high wall and only one entrance. Inside the wall was a courtyard with a stable for a pony and a byre for two cows, the house itself forming one side of the enclosure. When the heavy door of the courtyard was closed, the *bania's* money bags were safe within his little fort. It was only after the old man's death that a police post was established at Ahirpur.'

'So Ram Das had a police post as well as a fort?'

'The police offered him no protection. He was so mean that not a litre of oil or pinch of salt ever came from him to the police post. Naturally, we wasted no love on him. The people of Ahirpur hated and feared him, for most of them were in his debt and practically his slaves.

'Now when the time came for Dilawar Singh to pay the remaining two hundred and fifty rupees for his mare Leila, he went to Ram Das for a loan. He expected to be well squeezed in the way of interest, but to his great surprise and anger the *bania* refused to let him have the money on any terms. It looked as though Dilawar would have to return the mare and be content with some knock-kneed *ekka*-pony.

'A few days before the date of payment, Dilawar Singh had to visit a village some five miles down-stream to investigate a case. He took me with him. On our return journey that night a terrific thunder-storm compelled us to take shelter in a small hut in the forest. When at last the storm was over, we continued on our way, I on foot, and Dilawar Singh riding Leila. All the way he cursed his ill-luck at having to part with Leila, and called down curses on Ram Das. We were not far from the *bania's* house when the full moon, high in the sky, came out from behind the passing storm-clouds, and suddenly Leila shied violently at something white on the bank of the stream.

'It was the naked body of a dead man. It had either been pushed into the stream without burning or swept off the pyre by the swollen torrent. I was about to push it off into the stream when Dilawar stopped me, saying that the corpse which had frightened Leila might yet be able to save her.'

'Together we pulled the body a little way up the bank; then, after tying the mare to a tree, we carried the corpse up to the *bania's* house and propped it against the main doorway. Returning to the stream. Dilawar remounted Leila, and we concealed ourselves in the forest. Like everyone else in the village, we knew the *bania* was an early riser, always the first to leave his house and complete his morning ablutions.

'We sat and waited. The faint light of dawn was just beginning to make things visible when we heard the *bania's* courtyard door open. There was a thud, an exclamation, and then a long silence.'

'What had happened?'

'Ram Das had opened the door, and the corpse had fallen upon him! He was frightened almost out of his wits. That some enemy was responsible for the presence of the corpse he quickly realized, but how to rid himself of it? The stream! Even to touch the corpse was defilement, but, as the saying goes, "where there are no eyes, there is no caste"—and he began to drag the body along the river bank, panting and perspiring, yet cold with terror. He had almost reached the stream when we emerged casually from our shelter.

' "Ah, *bania-ji* you are up early this morning!" called Dilawar Singh. "Hullo, what's this? Is this one of your unfortunate debtors? Have you taken his life as well as his clothes?"

Ram Das fell on his knees. His voice failed, and he went as pale as the corpse he still held by the feet. Dilawar Singh dismounted, caught him roughly by the arm and dragged him to his feet.

' "*Thanadar sahib*, I will let you have the money," gasped Ram Das.

' "What money?"

' "The two hundred and fifty rupees you wanted last week."

' "Then hurry up," said Dilawar Singh, "or someone will come, and I shall be compelled to arrest you. Run!"

'The unfortunate Ram Das realized that he was in an evil predicament. True, he was innocent, but before he could prove this he would be arrested by the police whom he had scorned and flouted—lawyers would devour his savings—he would be torn from his family and deprived of his comforts—and worst of all, his clients would delay repayments! After only a little hesitation, he ran to his house and returned with two hundred and fifty rupees, which he handed over to Dilawar Singh. And, as far as I know—for I was transferred from Ahirpur a few weeks later—he never asked Dilawar Singh for its return.'

'And what of the body?' I asked.

'We pushed it back into the stream,' said Ghanshyam. 'It had served its purpose well. Nathu, do you insist that a dead man is no good to anyone?'

'No good at all,' said Nathu, spitting into the fire's fast fading glow. 'For I came to Ahirpur not long after you were transferred. I had the pleasure of meeting *thanadar* Dilawar Singh, and seeing his fine mare. It is true that he had the *bania* under his thumb, for Ram Das provided all the feed for the mare, at no charge. But one day the mare had a fit while Dilawar Singh was riding her, and plunging about in the street, flung her master to the ground with a broken neck. She was indeed a dead man's gift!'

'The *bania* must have been quite pleased at the turn of events,' I said.

'Some say he poisoned the mare's feed. Anyway, he kept the police happy by providing the oil to light poor Dilawar Singh's funeral pyre, and generously refused to accept any payment for it!'

Whispering in the Dark

A wild night, wind moaning, trees lashing themselves in a frenzy, rain spurting up from the road, thunder over the mountains. Loneliness stretched ahead of me, a loneliness of the heart as well as a physical loneliness. The world was blotted out by a mist that had come up from the valley, a thick white clammy shroud.

I groped through the forest, groped in my mind for the memory of a mountain path, some remembered rock or ancient deodar. Then a streak of blue lightning gave me a glimpse of barren hillside and a house cradled in mist.

It was an old-world house, built of limestone rock on the outskirts of a crumbling hill-station. There was no light in its windows; probably the electricity had been disconnected long ago. But, if I could get in, it would do for the night.

I had no torch, but at times the moon shone through the wild clouds, and trees loomed out of the mist like primeval giants. I reached the front door and found it locked from within; walked round to the side and broke a window-pane; put my hand through shattered glass and found the bolt.

The window, warped by over a hundred monsoons, resisted at first. When it yielded, I climbed into the mustiness of a long-closed room, and the wind came in with me, scattering papers across the floor and knocking some unidentifiable object off a table. I closed the window, bolted it again; but the mist crawled through the broken glass, and the wind rattled in it like a pair of castanets.

There were matches in my pocket. I struck three before a light flared up.

I was in a large room, crowded with furniture. Pictures on the walls. Vases on the mantelpiece. A candlestand. And, strangely enough, no cobwebs. For all its external look of neglect and dilapidation, the house had been cared for by someone. But

118

before I could notice anything else, the match burnt out.

As I stepped further into the room, the old deodar flooring creaked beneath my weight. By the light of another match I reached the mantle-piece and lit the candle, noticing at the same time that the candlestick was a genuine antique with cutglass hangings. A deserted cottage with good furniture and glass. I wondered why no one had ever broken in. And then realized that I had just done so.

I held the candlestick high and glanced round the room. The walls were hung with several water-colours and portraits in oils. There was no dust anywhere. But no one answered my call, no one responded to my hesitant knocking. It was as though the occupants of the house were in hiding, watching me obliquely from dark corners and chimneys.

I entered a bedroom and found myself facing a full-length mirror. My reflection stared back at me as though I were a stranger, as though it (the reflection) belonged to the house, while I was only an outsider.

As I turned from the mirror, I thought I saw someone, something, some reflection other than mine, move behind me in the mirror. I caught a glimpse of whiteness, a pale oval face, burning eyes, long tresses, golden in the candlelight. But when I looked in the mirror again there was nothing to be seen but my own pallid face.

A pool of water was forming at my feet. I set the candle down on a small table, found the edge of the bed—a large old four-poster—sat down, and removed my soggy shoes and socks. Then I took off my clothes and hung them over the back of a chair.

I stood naked in the darkness, shivering a little. There was no one to see me—and yet I felt oddly exposed, almost as though I had stripped in a room full of curious people.

I got under the bedclothes—they smelt slightly of eucalyptus and lavender—but found there was no pillow. That was odd. A perfectly made bed, but no pillow! I was too tired to hunt for one. So I blew out the candle—and the darkness closed in around me, and the whispering began. . . .

The whispering began as soon as I closed my eyes. I couldn't tell where it came from. It was all around me, mingling with the sound of the wind coughing in the chimney, the stretching of old furniture, the weeping of trees outside in the rain.

Sometimes I could hear what was being said. The words came from a distance: a distance, not so much of space, as of time. .

'Mine, mine, he is all mine. . . .'

'He is ours, dear, ours.'

Whispers, echoes, words hovering around me with bat's wings, saying the most inconsequential things with a logical urgency. 'You're late for supper....'

'He lost his way in the mist.'

'Do you think he has any money?'

'To kill a turtle you must first tie its legs to two posts.'

'We could tie him to the bed and pour boiling water down his throat.'

'No, it's simpler this way.'

I sat up. Most of the whispering had been distant, impersonal, but this last remark had sounded horribly near.

I relit the candle and the voices stopped. I got up and prowled around the room, vainly looking for some explanation for the voices. Once again I found myself facing the mirror, staring at my own reflection and the reflection of that other person, the girl with the golden hair and shining eyes. And this time she held a pillow in her hands. She was standing behind me.

I remembered then the stories I had heard as a boy, of two spinster sisters—one beautiful, one plain—who lured rich, elderly gentlemen into their boarding-house and suffocated them in the night. The deaths had appeared quite natural, and they had got away with it for years. It was only the surviving sister's death-bed confession that had revealed the truth—and even then no one had believed her.

But that had been many, many years ago, and the house had long since fallen down. . . . .

When I turned from the mirror, there was no one behind me. I looked again, and the reflection had gone.

I crawled back into the bed and put the candle out. And I slept and dreamt (or was I awake and did it really happen?) that the women I had seen in the mirror stood beside the bed, leant over me, looked at me with eyes flecked by orange flames. I saw people moving in those eyes. I saw myself. And then her lips touched mine, lips so cold, so dry, that a shudder ran through my body.

And then, while her face became faceless and only the eyes remained, something else continued to press down upon me, something soft, heavy and shapeless, enclosing me in a suffocating embrace. I could not turn my head or open my mouth, I could not breathe.

I raised my hands and clutched feebly at the thing on top of me. And to my surprise it came away; It was only a pillow that had somehow fallen over my face, half suffocating me while I dreamt of a phantom kiss.

I flung the pillow aside. I flung the bedclothes from me. I had had enough of whispering, of ownerless reflections, of pillows and that fell on me in the dark, I would brave the storm outside rather than continue to seek rest in this tortured house.

I dressed quickly. The candle had almost guttered out. The house and everything in it belonged to the darkness of another time; I belonged to the light of day.

I was ready to leave. I avoided the tall mirror with its grotesque rococo design. Holding the candlestick before me, I moved cautiously into the front room. The pictures on the walls sprang to life.

One, in particular, held my attention, and I moved closer to examine it more carefully by the light of the dwindling candle. Was it just my imagination, or was the girl in the portrait the woman of my dream, the beautiful pale reflection in the mirror? Had I gone back in time, or had time caught up with me? Is it time that's passing by, or is it you and I?

I turned to leave. And the candle gave one final sputter and went out, plunging the room in darkness. I stood still for a moment, trying to collect my thoughts, to still the panic that came rushing upon me. Just then there was a knocking on the door.

'Who's there?' I called.

Silence. And then, again, the knocking, and this time a voice, low and insistent: 'Please let me in, please let me in....'

I stepped forward, unbolted the door, and flung it open.

She stood outside in the rain. Not the pale, beautiful one, but a wizened old hag with bloodless lips and flaring nostrils and— but where were the eyes? No eyes, no eyes!

She swept past me on the wind, and at the same time I took advantage of the open doorway to run outside, to run gratefully into the pouring rain, to be lost for hours among the dripping trees, to be glad of the leeches clinging to my flesh.

And when, with the dawn, I found my way at last, I rejoiced in bird-song and the sunlight piercing scattering clouds.

And today, if you were to ask me if the old house is still there or not, I would not be able to tell you, for the simple reason that I haven't the slightest desire to go looking for it.

He Said it with Arsenic

Is there such a person as a born murderer—in the sense that there are born writers and musicians, born winners and losers?

One can't be sure. The urge to do away with troublesome people is common to most of us, but only a few succumb to it.

If ever there was a born murderer, he must surely have been William Jones. The thing came so naturally to him. No extreme violence, no messy shootings or hackings or throttling; just the right amount of poison, administered with skill and discretion.

A gentle, civilized sort of person was Mr Jones. He collected butterflies and arranged them systematically in glass cases. His ether bottle was quick and painless. He never stuck pins into the beautiful creatures.

Have you ever heard of the Agra Double Murder? It happened, of course, a great many years ago, when Agra was a far-flung outpost of the British Empire. In those days, William Jones was a male nurse in one of the city's hospitals. The patients—especially terminal cases—spoke highly of the care and consideration he showed them. While most nurses, both male and female, preferred to attend to the more hopeful cases, nurse William was always prepared to stand duty over a dying patient.

He felt a certain empathy for the dying; he liked to see them on their way. It was just his good nature, of course.

On a visit to nearby Meerut, he met and fell in love with Mrs Browning, the wife of the local station-master. Impassioned love letters were soon putting a strain on the Agra-Meerut postal service. The envelopes grew heavier—not so much because the letters were growing longer but because they contained little packets of a powdery white substance, accompanied by detailed instructions as to its correct administration.

Mr Browning, an unassuming and trustful man—one of the world's born losers, in fact—was not the sort to read his wife's correspondence. Even when he was seized by frequent attacks of colic, he put them down to an impure water supply. He recovered from one bout of vomitting and diarrohea only to be racked by another.

He was hospitalized on a diagnosis of gastroentritis; and, thus freed from his wife's ministrations, soon got better. But on returning home and drinking a glass of *nimbu-pani* brought to him by the solicitous Mrs Browning, he had a relapse from which he did not recover.

Those were the days when deaths from cholera and related diseases were only too common in India, and death certificates were easier to obtain than dog licences.

After a short interval of mourning (it was the hot weather and you couldn't wear black for long), Mrs Browning moved to Agra, where she rented a house next door to William Jones.

I forgot to mention that Mr Jones was also married. His wife was an insignificant creature, no match for a genius like William. Before the hot weather was over, the dreaded cholera had taken her too. The way was clear for the lovers to unite in holy matrimony.

But Dame Gossip lived in Agra too, and it was not long before tongues were wagging and anonymous letters were being received by the Superintendent of Police. Enquiries were instituted. Like most infatuated lovers, Mrs Browning had hung on to her beloved's letters and billet-doux, and these soon came to light. The silly woman had kept them in a box beneath her bed.

Exhumations were ordered in both Agra and Meerut.

Arsenic keeps well, even in the hottest of weather, and there was no dearth of it in the remains of both victims.

Mr Jones and Mrs Browning were arrested and charged with murder.

*

'Is Uncle Bill really a murderer?' I asked from the drawing room sofa in my grandmother's house in Dehra. (It's time that I told you that William Jones was my uncle, my mother's half-brother.)

I was eight or nine at the time. Uncle Bill had spent the previous summer with us in Dehra and had stuffed me with bazaar sweets and pastries, all of which I had consumed without suffering any ill effects.

'Who told you that about Uncle Bill?' asked Grandmother.

'I heard it in school. All the boys were asking me the same question—"Is your uncle a murderer?" They say he poisoned both his wives.'

'He had only one wife,' snapped Aunt Mabel.

'Did he poison her?'

'No, of course not. How can you say such a thing!'

'Then why is Uncle Bill in gaol?'

'Who says he's in gaol?'

'The boys at school. They heard it from their parents. Uncle Bill is to go on trial in the Agra fort.'

There was a pregnant silence in the drawing room, then Aunt Mabel burst out: 'It was all that awful woman's fault.'

'Do you mean Mrs Browning?' asked Grandmother.

'Yes, of course. She must have put him up to it. Bill couldn't have thought of anything so—so diabolical!'

'But he sent her the powders, dear. And don't forget—Mrs Browning has since. . . .'

Grandmother stopped in mid-sentence, and both she and Aunt Mabel glanced surreptitiously at me.

'Committed suicide,' I filled in. 'There were still some powders with her.'

Aunt Mabel's eyes rolled heaven-wards. 'This boy is impossible. I don't know what he will be like when he grows up.'

'At least I won't be like Uncle Bill,' I said. 'Fancy poisoning people! If I kill anyone, it will be in a fair fight. I suppose they'll hang Uncle?'

'Oh, I hope not!'

Grandmother was silent. Uncle Bill was her step-son but she did have a soft spot for him. Aunt Mabel, his sister, thought he was wonderful. I had always considered him to be a bit soft but had to admit that he was generous. I tried to imagine him dangling at the end of a hangman's rope, but somehow he didn't fit the picture.

As things turned out, he didn't hang. White people in India seldom got the death sentence, although the hangman was pretty busy disposing off dacoits and political terrorists. Uncle

Bill was given a life-sentence and settled down to a sedentary job in the prison library at Naini, near Allahabad. His gifts as a male nurse went unappreciated; they did not trust him in the hospital.

He was released after seven or eight years, shortly after the country became an independent Republic. He came out of gaol to find that the British were leaving, either for England or the remaining colonies. Grandmother was dead. Aunt Mabel and her husband had settled in South Africa. Uncle Bill realized that there was little future for him in India and followed his sister out to Johannesburg. I was in my last year at boarding school. After my father's death, my mother had married an Indian, and now my future lay in India.

I did not see Uncle Bill after his release from prison, and no one dreamt that he would ever turn up again in India.

In fact, fifteen years were to pass before he came back, and by then I was in my early thirties, the author of a book that had become something of a best-seller. The previous fifteen years had been a struggle—the sort of struggle that every young freelance writer experiences—but at last the hard work was paying off and the royalties were beginning to come in.

I was living in a small cottage on the outskirts of the hill-station of Fosterganj, working on another book, when I received an unexpected visitor.

He was a thin, stooped, grey-haired man in his late fifties, with a straggling moustache and discoloured teeth. He looked feeble and harmless but for his eyes which were pale cold blue. There was something slightly familiar about him.

'Don't you remember me?' he asked. 'Not that I really expect you to, after all these years. . . .'

'Wait a minute. Did you teach me at school?'

'No—but you're getting warm.' He put his suitcase down and I glimpsed his name on the airlines label. I looked up in astonishment. 'You're not—you couldn't be. . . .'

'Your Uncle Bill,' he said with a grin and extended his hand. 'None other!' And he sauntered into the house.

I must admit that I had mixed feelings about his arrival. While I had never felt any dislike for him, I hadn't exactly approved of what he had done. Poisoning, I felt, was a particularly reprehensible way of getting rid of inconvenient people: not that I could think of any commendable ways of getting rid of them! Still, it had happened a long time ago, he'd been punished, and presumably he was a reformed character.

'And what have you been doing all these years?' he asked me, easing himself into the only comfortable chair in the room.

'Oh just writing,' I said.

'Yes, I heard about your last book. It's quite a success, isn't it?'

'It's doing quite well. Have you read it?'

'I don't do much reading.'

'And what have you been doing all these years, Uncle Bill?'

'Oh, knocking about here and there. Worked for a soft drink company for some time. And then with a drug firm. My knowledge of chemicals was useful.'

'Weren't you with Aunt Mabel in South Africa?'

'I saw quite a lot of her, until she died a couple of years ago. Didn't you know?'

'No. I've been out of touch with relatives.' I hoped he'd take that as a hint. 'And what about her husband?'

'Died too, not long after. Not many of us left, my boy. That's why, when I saw something about you in the papers, I thought—why not go and see my only nephew again?'

'You're welcome to stay a few days,' I said quickly. 'Then I have to go to Bombay.' (This was a lie, but I did not relish the prospect of looking after Uncle Bill for the rest of his days.)

'Oh, I won't be staying long,' he said. 'I've got a bit of money put by in Johannesburg. It's just that—so far as I know—you're my only living relative, and I thought it would be nice to see you again.'

Feeling relieved, I set about trying to make Uncle Bill as comfortable as possible. I gave him my bedroom and turned the window-seat into a bed for myself. I was a hopeless cook but, using all my ingenuity, I scrambled some eggs for supper. He waved aside my apologies; he'd always been a frugal eater, he said. Eight years in gaol had given him a cast-iron stomach.

He did not get in my way but left me to my writing and my lonely walks. He seemed content to sit in the spring sunshine and smoke his pipe.

It was during our third evening together that he said, 'Oh, I almost forgot. There's a bottle of sherry, in my suitcase. I brought it especially for you.'

'That was very thoughtful of you, Uncle Bill. How did you know I was fond of sherry?'

'Just my intutition. You do like it, don't you?'

'There's nothing like a good sherry.'

He went to his bedroom and came back with an unopened bottle of South African sherry.

'Now you just relax near the fire,' he said agreeably. 'I'll open the bottle and fetch glasses.'

He went to the kitchen while I remained near the electric fire, flipping through some journals. It seemed to me that Uncle bill was taking rather a long time. Intuition must be a family trait, because it came to me quite suddenly—the thought that Uncle Bill might be intending to poison me.

After all, I thought, here he is after nearly fifteen years, apparently for purely sentimental reasons. But I had just published a best-seller. And I was his nearest relative. If I was to die, Uncle Bill could lay claim to my estate and probably live comfortably on my royalties for the next five or six years!

What had really happened to Aunt Mabel and her husband, I wondered. And where did Uncle Bill get the money for an air ticket to India?

Before I could ask myself any more questions, he reappeared with the glasses on a tray. He set the tray on a small table that stood between us. The glasses had been filled. The sherry sparkled.

I stared at the glass nearest me, trying to make out if the liquid in it was cloudier than that in the other glass. But there appeared to be no difference.

I decided I would not take any chances. It was a round tray, made of smooth Kashmiri walnut wood. I turned it round with my index finger, so that the glasses changed places.

'Why did you do that?' asked Uncle Bill.

'It's a custom in these parts. You turn the tray with the sun, a complete revolution. It brings good luck.'

Uncle Bill looked thoughtful for a few moments, then said, 'Well, let's have some more luck,' and turned the tray around again.

'Now you've spoilt it,' I said. 'You're not supposed to keep revolving it! That's bad luck. I'll have to turn it about again to cancel out the bad luck.'

The tray swung round once more, and Uncle Bill had the glass that was meant for me.

'Cheers!' I said, and drank from my glass.

It was good sherry.

Uncle Bill hesitated. Then he shrugged, said 'Cheers', and drained his glass quickly.

But he did not offer to fill the glasses again.

Early next morning he was taken violently ill. I heard him retching in his room, and I got up and went to see if there was anything I could do. He was groaning, his head hanging over the side of the bed. I brought him a basin and a jug of water.

'Would you like me to fetch a doctor?' I asked.

He shook his head. 'No I'll be all right. It must be something I ate.'

'It's probably the water. It's not too good at this time of the year. Many people come down with gastric trouble during their first few days in Fosterganj.'

'Ah, that must be it,' he said, and doubled up as a fresh spasm of pain and nausea swept over him.

He was better by evening—whatever had gone into the glass must have been by way of the preliminary dose and a day later he was well enough to pack his suitcase and announce his departure. The climate of Fosterganj did not agree with him, he told me.

Just before he left, I said: 'Tell me, Uncle, why did you drink it?'

'Drink what? The water?'

'No, the glass of sherry into which you'd slipped one of your famous powders.'

He gaped at me, then gave a nervous whinnying laugh. 'You will have your little joke, won't you?'

'No, I mean it,' I said. 'Why did you drink the stuff? It was meant for me, of course.'

He looked down at his shoes, then gave a little shrug and turned away.

'In the circumstances,' he said, 'it seemed the only decent thing to do.'

I'll say this for Uncle Bill: he was always the perfect gentleman.

129

The Most Potent Medicine of All

Like most men, Wang Chei was fond of being his own doctor. He studied the book of the ancient physician Lu Fei whenever he felt slightly indisposed. Had he really been familiar with the peculiarities of his digestion, he would have avoided eating too many pickled prawns. But he ate pickled prawns first, and studied Lu Fei afterward.

Lu Fei, a physician of renown in Yunnan during the twelth century, had devoted eight chapters to disorders of the belly, and there are many in western China who still swear by his methods—just as there are many in England who still swear by Culpepper's Herbal.

The great physician was a firm believer in the potency of otters' tails, and had Wang Chei taken a dose of otters' tails the morning after the prawns, his pain and cramps might soon have disappeared.

But otters' tails are both rare and expensive. In order to obtain a tail, one must catch an otter; in order to catch an otter, one must find a river; and there were no rivers in the region where Wang Chei lived.

Wang grew potatoes to sell in the market twelve miles away, and sometimes he traded in opium. But what interested him most was the practice of medicine, and he had some reputation as a doctor among those villagers who regarded the distant hospital with suspicion.

And so, in the absence of otters' tails, he fell back upon the gall of bear, the fat of python, the whiskers of tiger, the blood of rhino, and the horn of sambar in velvet. He tried all these (he had them in stock), mixing them—as directed by the book of Lu Fei—in the water of melted hailstones.

Wang took all these remedies in turn, anxiously noting the reactions that took place in his system. Unfortunately, neither he nor his mentor, Lu Fei, had given much thought to diagnosis, and he did not associate his trouble with the pickled prawns.

Life would hardly have been worth living without a few indulgences, especially as Wang's wife excelled at making pickles. This was his misfortune. Her pickles were such that no man could refuse them.

She was devoted to Wang Chei and indulged his tastes and his enormous appetite. Like him, she occasionally dipped into the pages of Lu Fei. From them she had learned that mutton fat was good for the eyebrows and that raspberry-leaf tea was just the thing for expectant mothers.

Her faith in this physician of an earlier century was as strong as her husband's. And now, with Wang Chei groaning and tossing on his bed, she studied the chapters on abdominal complaints.

It appeared to her that Wang was very ill indeed, and she did not connect his woeful condition with over-indulgence. He had been in bed for two days. Had he not dosed himself so liberally with python's fat and rhino's blood, it is possible that he might have recovered on the morning following his repast. Now he was too ill to mix himself any further concoctions. Fortunately—as he supposed—his wife was there to continue the treatment.

She was a small pale woman who moved silently about the house on little feet. It was difficult to believe that this frail creature had brought eleven healthy children into the world. Her husband had once been a strong, handsome man; but now the skin under his eyes was crinkling, his cheeks were hollow, his once well-proportioned body was sagging with loose flesh.

Nevertheless, Wang's wife loved him with the same intensity as on the day they first fell in love, twenty years ago. Anxiously, she turned the pages of Lu Fei.

Wang was not as critically ill as she imagined; but she was frightened by his distorted features, his sweating body, his groans of distress. Watching him lying there, helpless and in agony, she could not help remembering the slim, virile husband of her youth; she was overcome with pity and compassion.

And then she discovered, in the book of Lu Fei, a remedy for his disorder that could be resorted to when all else had failed.

It was around midnight when she prepared the vital potion—a potion prepared with selfless love and compassion. And it was almost dawn when, weak and exhausted, she brought him the potion mixed in a soup.

Wang felt no inclination for a bowl of soup at 5 a.m. He had with difficulty snatched a few hours of sleep, and his wife's interruption made him irritable.

'Must I drink this filth?' he complained. 'What is it anyway?'

'Never mind what it is,' she coaxed. 'It will give you strength and remove your pain.'

'But what's in it?' persisted Wang. 'Of what is it made?'

'Of love,' said his wife. 'It is recommended in the book of Lu Fei. He says it is the best of all remedies, and cannot fail.' She held the bowl to her husband's lips.

He drank hurriedly to get it over with, and only when he was halfway through the bowl did he suspect that something was wrong. It was his wife's terrible condition that made him sit up in bed, thrusting the bowl away. A terrible suspicion formed in his mind.

'Do not deceive me,' he demanded. 'Tell me at once—what is this potion made of?'

She told him then; and when Wang Chei heard her confession, he knelt before his wife who had by now collapsed on the floor. Seizing the hurricane lantern, he held it to her. Her body was wrapped in a towel, but from her left breast, the region of the heart, blood was oozing through the heavy cloth.

She had read in the book of Lu Fei that only her own flesh and blood could cure her husband; and these she had unflinchingly taken from her soft and generous bosom.

You were right, Lu Fei, old sage. What more potent ingredients are there than love and compassion?

Hanging at the Mango-Tope

The two captive policemen, Inspector Hukam Singh and Sub-Inspector Guler Singh, were being pushed unceremoniously along the dusty, deserted, sun-drenched road. The people of the village had made themselves scarce. They would reappear only when the dacoits went away.

The leader of the dacoit gang was Mangal Singh Bundela, great-grandson of a Pindari adventurer who had been a thorn in the side of the British. Mangal was doing his best to be a thorn in the flesh of his own Government. The local police force had been strengthened recently but it was still inadequate for dealing with the dacoits who knew the ravines better than any surveyor. The dacoit Mangal had made a fortune out of ransom: his chief victims were the sons of wealthy industrialists, money-lenders or landowners. But today he had captured two police officials; of no value as far as ransom went, but prestigious prisoners who could be put to other uses. . . .

Mangal Singh wanted to show off in front of the police. He would kill at least one of them—his reputation demanded it—but he would let the other go, in order that his legendary power and ruthlessness be given a maximum publicity. A legend is always a help!

His red and green turban was tied rakishly to one side. His dhoti extended right down to his ankles. His slippers were embroidered with gold and silver thread. His weapon was no ancient matchlock, but a well-greased .303 rifle. Two of his men had similar rifles. Some had revolvers. Only the smaller fry carried swords or country-made pistols. Mangal Singh's gang, though traditional in many ways, was up-to-date in the matter of weapons. Right now they had the policemen's guns too.

'Come along, Inspector *sahib*,' said Mangal Singh, in tones of police barbarity, tugging at the rope that encircled the stout Inspector's midriff. 'Had you captured me today, you would have been a hero. You would have taken all the credit, even though you could not keep up with your men in the ravines. Too bad you chose to remain sitting in your jeep with the Sub-Inspector. The jeep will be useful to us, you will not. But I would like you to be a hero all the same—and there is none better than a dead hero!'

Mangal Singh's followers doubled up with laughter. They loved their leader's cruel sense of humour.

'As for you, Guler Singh,' he continued, giving his attention to the Sub-Inspector, 'You are a man from my own village. You should have joined me long ago. But you were never to be trusted. You thought there would be better pickings in the police, didn't you?'

Guler Singh said nothing, simply hung his head and wondered what his fate would be. He felt certain that Mangal Singh would devise some diabolical and fiendish method of dealing with his captives. Guler Singh's only hope was Constable Ghanshyam, who hadn't been caught by the dacoits because, at the time of the ambush, he had been in the bushes relieving himself.

'To the mango-tope!' said Mangal Singh, prodding the policemen forward.

'Listen to me, Mangal,' said the perspiring Inspector, who was ready to try anything to get out of his predicament. 'Let me go, and I give you my word there'll be no trouble for you in this area as long as I am posted here. What could be more convenient than that?'

'Nothing,' said Mangal Singh. 'But your word isn't good. *My* word is different. I have told my men that I will hang you at the mango-tope, and I mean to keep my word. But I believe in fair-play—I like a little sport! You may yet go free if your friend here, Sub-Inspector Guler Singh, has his wits about him.'

The Inspector and his subordinate exchanged doubtful puzzled looks. They were not to remain puzzled for long. On reaching the mango-tope, the dacoits produced a good strong hempen rope, one end looped into a slip-knot. Many a garland of marigolds had the Inspector received during his mediocre career. Now, for the first time, he was being garlanded with a hangman's noose. He had seen hangings; he had rather enjoyed them; but he had no stomach for his own. The Inspector begged for mercy. Who wouldn't have in his position?'

'Be quiet,' commanded Mangal Singh. 'I do not want to know about your wife and your children and the manner in which they will starve. You shot my son last year.'

'Not I!' cried the Inspector. 'It was some other.'

'You led the party. But now, just to show you that I'm a sporting fellow, I am going to have you strung up from this tree, and then I am going to give Guler Singh six shots with a rifle, and if he can sever the rope that suspends you before you are dead, well then, you can remain alive and I will let you go! For your sake, I hope the Sub-Inspector's aim is good. He will have to shoot fast. My man Phambiri, who has made this noose, was once executioner in a city jail. He guarantees that you won't last more than fifteen seconds at the end of *his* rope.

Guler Singh was taken to a spot about forty yards. A rifle was thrust into his hands. Two dacoits clambered into the branches of the mango tree. The Inspector, his hands tied behind, could only gaze at them in horror. His mouth opened and shut as though he already had need of more air. And then, suddenly, the rope went taut, up went the Inspector, his throat caught in a vice, while the branch of the tree shook and mango-blossoms fluttered to the ground The Inspector dangled from the rope, his feet about three feet above the ground.

'You can shoot,' said Mangal Singh, nodding to the Sub-Inspector.

And Guler Singh his hands trembling a little, raised the rifle to his shoulder and fired three shots in rapid succession. But the rope was swinging violently and the Inspector's body was jerking about like a fish on a hook. The bullets went wide.

Guler Singh found the magazine empty. He reloaded, wiped the stinging sweat from his eyes, raised the rifle again, took more careful aim. His hands were steadier now. He rested the sights on the upper portion of the rope, where there was less motion. Normally he was a good shot, but he had never been asked to demonstrate his skill in circumstances such as these.

The Inspector still gyrated at the end of his rope. There was life in him yet. His face was purple. The world, in those choking moments, was a medley of upside-down roofs and a red sun spinning slowly towards him.

Guler Singh's rifle cracked again. An inch or two wide this

time. But the fifth shot found its mark, sending small tuffs of rope winging into the air.

The shot did not sever the rope; it was only a nick.

Guler Singh had one shot left. He was quite calm. The rifle-sight followed the rope's swing, less agitated now that the Inspector's convulsions were lessening. Guler Singh felt sure he could sever the rope this time.

And then, as his finger touched the trigger, an odd, disturbing thought slipped into his mind, hung there, throbbing: 'Whose life are you trying to save? Hukam Singh has stood in the way of your promotion more than once. He had you charge-sheeted for accepting fifty rupees from an unlicensed rickshaw-puller. He makes you do all the dirty work, blames you when things go wrong, takes the credit when there is credit to be taken. But for him, you'd be an Inspector!'

The rope swayed slightly to the right. The rifle moved just a fraction to the left. The last shot rang out, clipping a sliver of bark from the mango tree.

The Inspector was dead when they cut him down.

'Bad luck,' said Mangal Singh Bundela. 'You nearly saved him. But the next time I catch up with you, Guler Singh, it will be your turn to hang from the mango tree. So keep well away! You know that I am a man of my word. I keep it now, by giving you your freedom.'

A few minutes later the party of dacoits had melted away into the late afternoon shadows of the scrub forest. There was the sound of a jeep starting up. Then silence—a silence so profound that it seemed to be shouting in Guler Singh's ears.

As the village people began to trickle out of their houses, Constable Ghanshyam appeared as if from nowhere, swearing that he had lost his way in the jungle. Several people had seen the incident from their windows; they were unanimous in praising the Sub-Inspector for his brave attempt to save his superior's life. He had done his best.

'It is true,' thought Guler Singh. 'I did my best.'

That moment of hesitation before the last shot, the question that had suddenly reared up in the darkness of his mind, had already gone from his memory. We remember only what we want to remember.

'I did my best,' he told everyone.

And so he had.

Eyes of the Cat

Her eyes seemed flecked with gold when the sun was on them. And as the sun set over the mountains, drawing a deep red wound across the sky, there was more than gold in Binya's eyes, there was anger; for she had been cut to the quick by some remarks her teacher had made—the culmination of weeks of insults and taunts.

Binya was poorer than most of the girls in her class and could not afford the tuitions that had become almost obligatory if one was to pass and be promoted. 'You'll have to spend another year in the 9th,' said Madam. 'And if you don't like that, you can find another school—a school where it won't matter if your blouse is torn and your tunic is old and your shoes are falling apart.' Madam had shown her large teeth in what was supposed to be a good-natured smile, and all the girls had tittered dutifully. Sycophancy had become part of the curriculum, in Madam's private academy for girls.

On the way home in the gathering gloom, Binya's two companions commiserated with her.

'She's a mean old thing,' said Usha. 'She doesn't care for anyone but herself.'

'Her laugh reminds me of a donkey braying,' said Sunita, who was more forthright.

But Binya wasn't really listening. Her eyes were fixed on some point in the far distance, where the pines stood in silhouette against a night sky that was growing brighter every moment. The moon was rising, a full moon, a moon that meant something very special to Binya, that made her blood tingle and her skin prickle and her hair glow and send out sparks. Her steps seemed to grow lighter, her limbs more sinewy as she moved gracefully, softly over the mountain path.

Abruptly she left her companions at a fork in the road.

'I'm taking the short cut through the forest,' she said.

Her friends were used to her sudden whims. They knew she was not afraid of being alone in the dark. But Binya's moods made them feel a little nervous, and now, holding hands, they hurried home along the open road.

The short cut took Binya through the dark oak forest. The crooked, tormented branches of the oaks threw twisted shadows across the path. A jackal howled at the moon; a nightjar called from the bushes. Binya walked fast, not out of fear but from urgency, and her breath came in short sharp gasps. Bright moonlight bathed the hillside when she reached her home on the outskirts of the village.

Refusing her dinner, she went straight to her small room and flung the window open. Moonbeams crept over the window-sill and over her arms which were already covered with golden hair. Her strong nails had shredded the rotten wood of the window-sill.

*

Tail swishing and ears pricked, the tawny leopard came swiftly out of the window, crossed the open field behind the house, and melted into the shadows.

A little later it padded silently through the forest.

Although the moon shone brightly on the tin-roofed town, the leopard knew where the shadows were deepest and emerged beautifully with them. An occasional intake of breath, which resulted in a short rasping cough, was the only sound it made.

Madam was returning from dinner at a ladies' club, called the Kitten Club as a sort of foil to their husbands' club affiliations. There were still a few people in the street, and while no one could help noticing Madam, who had the contours of a steam-roller, none saw or heard the predator who had slipped down a side alley and reached the steps of the teacher's house. It sat there silently, waiting with all the patience of an obedient schoolgirl.

When Madam saw the leopard on her steps, she dropped her handbag and opened her mouth to scream; but her voice would not materialize. Nor would her tongue ever be used again, either to savour chicken biryani or to pour scorn upon her pupils, for the leopard had sprung at her throat, broken her neck, and dragged her into the bushes.

*

In the morning, when Usha and Sunita set out for school, they stopped as usual at Binya's cottage and called out to her.

Binya was sitting in the sun, combing her long black hair.

'Aren't you coming to school today, Binya?' asked the girls.

'No, I won't bother to go today,' said Binya. She felt lazy, but pleased with herself, like a contented cat.

'Madam won't be pleased,' said Usha. 'Shall we tell her you're sick?'

'It won't be necessary,' said Binya, and gave them one of her mysterious smiles. 'I'm sure it's going to be a holiday.'

A Crow for All Seasons

Early to bed and early to rise makes a crow healthy, wealthy and wise.

They say it's true for humans too. I'm not so sure about that. But for crows it's a must.

I'm always up at the crack of dawn, often the first crow to break the night's silence with a lusty caw. My friends and relatives, who roost in the same tree, grumble a bit and mutter to themselves, but they are soon cawing just as loudly. Long before the sun is up, we set off on the day's work.

We do not pause even for the morning wash. Later in the day, if it's hot and muggy, I might take a dip in some human's bath water; but early in the morning we like to be up and about before everyone else. This is the time when trash cans and refuse dumps are overflowing with goodies, and we like to sift through them before the dustmen arrive in their disposal trucks.

Not that we are afraid of a famine in refuse. As human beings multiply, so does their rubbish.

Only yesterday I rescued an old typewriter ribbon from the dustbin, just before it was emptied. What a waste that would have been! I had no use for it myself, but I gave it to one of my cousins who got married recently, and she tells me it's just right for her nest, the one she's building on a telegraph pole. It helps her bind the twigs together, she says.

My own preference is for toothbrushes. They're just a hobby, really, like stamp-collecting with humans. I have a small but select collection which I keep in a hole in the garden wall. Don't ask me how many I've got—crows don't believe there's any point in counting beyond *two*— but I know there's more than *one*, that there's a whole lot of them in fact, because there isn't anyone living on this road who hasn't lost a toothbrush to me at some time or another.

We crows living in the jackfruit tree have this stretch of road to ourselves, but so that we don't quarrel or have misunderstandings we've shared the houses out. I picked the bungalow with the orchard at the back. After all, I don't eat rubbish and throw-aways all the time. Just occasionally I like a ripe guava or the soft flesh of a papaya. And sometimes I like the odd beetle as an *hors d'oeuvre*. Those humans in the bungalow should be grateful to me for keeping down the population of fruit-eating beetles, and even for recycling their refuse; but no, humans are never grateful. No sooner do I settle in one of their guava trees than stones are whizzing past me. So I return to the dustbin on the back veranda steps. They don't mind my being there.

One of my cousins shares the bungalow with me, but he's a lazy fellow and I have to do most of the foraging. Sometimes I get him to lend me a claw; but most of the time he's preening his feathers and trying to look handsome for a pretty young thing who lives in the banyan tree at the next turning.

When he's in the mood he can be invaluable, as he proved recently when I was having some difficulty getting at the dog's food on the veranda.

This dog who is fussed over so much by the humans I've adopted is a great big fellow, a mastiff who pretends to a pedigree going back to the time of Genghis Khan—he likes to pretend one of his ancestors was the great Khan's watchdog— but, as often happens in famous families, animal or human, there is a falling off in quality over a period of time, and this huge fellow—Tiger, they call him—is a case in point. All brawn and no brain. Many's the time I've removed a juicy bone from his plate or helped myself to pickings from under his nose.

But of late he's been growing canny and selfish. He doesn't like to share any more. And the other day I was almost in his jaws when he took a sudden lunge at me. Snap went his great teeth; but all he got was one of my tail feathers. He spat it out in disgust. Who wants crow's meat, anyway?

All the same, I thought, I'd better not be too careless. It's not for nothing that a crow's IQ is way above that of all other birds. And it's higher than a dog's, I bet.

*

I woke Cousin Slow from his midday siesta and said, 'Hey, Slow, we've got a problem. If you want any of that delicious tripe today, you've got to lend a claw—or a beak. That dog's getting snappier day by day.'

Slow opened one eye and said. 'Well, if you insist. But you know how I hate getting into a scuffle. It's bad for the gloss on my feathers.'

'I don't insist,' I said politely, 'but I'm not foraging for both of us today. It's every crow for himself.'

'Okay, okay, I'm coming,' said Slow, and with barely a flap he dropped down from the tree to the wall.

'What's the strategy?' I asked.

'Simple. We'll just give him the old one-two.'

We flew across to the veranda. Tiger had just started his meal. He was a fast, greedy eater who made horrible slurping sounds while he guzzled his food. We had to move fast if we wanted to get something before the meal was over.

I sidled up to Tiger and wished him good afternoon.

He kept on gobbling—but quicker now.

Slow came up from behind and gave him a quick peck near the tail—a sensitive spot—and, as Tiger swung round, snarling, I moved in quickly and snatched up several tidbits.

Tiger went for me, and I flew free-style for the garden wall. The dish was untended, so Slow helped himself to as many scraps as he could stuff in his mouth.

He joined me on the garden wall, and we sat there feasting, while Tiger barked himself hoarse below.

'Go catch a cat,' said Slow, who is given to slang. 'You're in the wrong league, big boy.'

The great sage Pratyasataka—ever heard of him? I guess not—once said, 'Nothing can improve a crow.'

Like most human sages, he wasn't very clear in his thinking, so that there has been some misunderstanding about what he meant. Humans like to think that what he really meant was that crows were so bad as to be beyond improvement. But we crows know better. We interpret the saying as meaning that the crow is so perfect that no improvement is possible.

It's not that we aren't human—what I mean is, there are times when we fall from our high standards and do rather foolish things. Like at lunch time the other day.

Sometimes, when the table is laid in the bungalow, and before the family enters the dining room, I nip in through the open window and make a quick foray among the dishes. Sometimes I'm lucky enough to pick up a sausage or a slice of toast, or even a pat of butter, making off before someone enters and throws a bread knife at me. But on this occasion, just as I was reaching for the toast, a thin slouching fellow—Junior *sahib* they call him—entered suddenly and shouted at me. I was so startled that I leapt across the table seeking shelter. Something flew at me, and in an effort to dodge the missile I put my head through a circular object and then found it wouldn't come off.

It wasn't safe to hang around there, so I flew out of window with this dashed ring still round my neck.

Serviette or napkin rings, that's what they are called. Quite unnecessary objects, but some humans—particularly the well-to-do sort—seem to like having them on their tables, holding bits of cloth in place. The cloth is used for wiping the mouth. Have you ever heard of such nonsense?

Anyway, there I was with a fat napkin ring round my neck, and as I perched on the wall trying to get it off, the entire human family gathered on their veranda to watch me.

There was the Colonel *sahib* and his wife, the *memsahib* ; there was the scrawny Junior *sahib* (worst of the lot); there was a mischievous boy (the Colonel *sahib's* grandson) known as the Baba; and there was the Cook (who usually flung orange peels at me) and the Gardener (who once tried to decapitate me with a spade), and the dog Tiger who, like most dogs, tries unsuccessfully to be a human.

Today they weren't cursing and shaking their fists at me; they were just standing and laughing their heads off. What's so funny about a crow with its head stuck in a napkin ring?

Worse was to follow.

The noise had attracted the other crows in the area, and if there's one thing crows detest, it's a crow who doesn't look like a crow.

They swooped low and dived on me, hammering at the wretched napkin ring, until they had knocked me off the wall and into a flower-bed. Then six or seven toughs landed on me with every intention of finishing me off.

'Hey, boys!' I cawed. 'This is me, Speedy! what are you trying to do—kill me?'

'That's right! You don't look like Speedy to us. What have you done with him, hey?'

And they set upon me with even greater vigour.

'You're just like a bunch of lousy humans!' I shouted. 'You're no better than them—this is just the way they carry on amongst themselves!'

That brought them to a halt. They stopped trying to peck me to pieces, and stood back, looking puzzled. The napkin ring had been shattered in the onslaught and had fallen to the ground.

'Why, it's Speedy!' said one of the gang.

'None other!'

'Good old Speedy—what are you doing here? And where's the guy we were hammering just now?'

There was no point in trying to explain things to them. Crows are like that. They're all good pals—until one of them tries to look different. Then he could be just another bird.

'He took off for Tibet,' I said. 'It was getting unhealthy for him around here.'

*

Summertime is here again. And although I'm a crow for all seasons, I must admit to a preference for the summer months.

Humans grow lazy and don't pursue me with so much vigour. Garbage cans overflow. Food goes bad and is constantly being thrown away. Overripe fruit gets tastier by the minute. If fellows like me weren't around to mop up all these unappreciated riches, how would humans manage?

There's one character in the bungalow, the Junior *sahib*, who will never appreciate our services, it seems. He simply hates crows. The small boy may throw stones at us occasionally, but then, he's the sort who throws stones at almost anything. There's nothing personal about it. He just throws stones on principle.

The *memsahib* is probably the best of the lot. She often throws me scraps from the kitchen—onionskins, potato peels, crusts, and leftovers—and even when I nip in and make off with something *not* meant for me (like a jam tart or a cheese *pakora*) she is quite sporting about it. The Junior *sahib* looks outraged, but the lady of the house says, 'Well, we've all got to make a living somehow, and that's how crows makes theirs. It's high time *you* thought of earning a living.' Junior *sahib's* her nephew—that's his occupation. He has never been known to work.

The Colonel *sahib* has a sense of humor but it's often directed at me. He thinks I'm a comedian.

He discovered I'd been making off with the occasional egg from the egg basket on the veranda, and one day, without my knowledge, he made a substitution.

Right on top of the pile I found a smooth round egg, and before anyone could shout 'Crow!' I'd made off with it. It was abnormally light. I put it down on the lawn and set about cracking it with my strong beak; but it would keep slipping away or bouncing off into the bushes. Finally I got it between my feet and gave it a good hard whack. It burst open, to my utter astonishment there was nothing inside!

I looked up and saw the old man standing on the veranda, doubled up with laughter.

'What are you laughing at?' asked the *memsahib*, coming out to see what it was all about.

'It's that ridiculous crow!' guffawed the Colonel, pointing at me. 'You know he's been stealing our eggs. Well, I placed a ping pong ball on top of the pile, and he fell for it! He's been struggling with that ball for twenty minutes! That will teach him a lesson.'

It did. But I had my revenge later, when I pinched a brand new toothbrush from the Colonel's bathroom.

*

The Junior *sahib* has no sense of humor at all. He idles about the house and grounds all day, whistling or singing to himself.

'Even that crow sings better than Uncle,' said the boy.

A truthful boy; but all he got for his honesty was a whack on the head from his uncle.

Anyway, as a gesture of appreciation, I perched on the garden wall and gave the family a rendering of my favourite crow song, which is my own composition. Here it is, translated for your benefit:

Oh, for the life of a crow!
A bird who's in the *know*.
Although we are cursed,
We are never dispersed—
We're always on the go!

I know I'm a bit of a rogue
(And my voice wouldn't pass for a brogue),
But there's no one as sleek
Or as neat with his beak—
So they're putting my picture in Vogue!

Oh, for the life of a crow!
I reap what I never sow,
They call me a thief—
Pray I'll soon come to grief—
But there's no getting rid of a crow!

I gave it everything I had, and the humans—all of them on the lawn to enjoy the evening breeze, listened to me in silence, struck with wonder at my performance.

When I had finished, I bowed and preened myself, waiting for the applause.

They stared at each other for a few seconds. Then the Junior *sahib* stooped, picked up a bottle opener, and flung it at me.

Well, I ask you!

What can one say about humans? I do my best to defend them from all kinds of criticism, and this is what I get for my pains.

Anyway, I picked up the bottle opener and added it to my collection of odds and ends.

It was getting dark, and soon everyone was stumbling around, looking for another bottle opener. Junior *sahib's* popularity was even lower than mine.

*

One day Junior *sahib* came home carrying a heavy shotgun. He pointed it at me a few times and I dived for cover. But he didn't fire. Probably I was out of range.

146

'He's only threatening you,' said Slow from the safety of the *jamun* tree, where he sat in the shadows. 'He probably doesn't know how to fire the thing.'

But I wasn't taking any chances. I'd seen a sly look on Junior *sahib's* face, and I decided that he was trying to make me careless. So I stayed well out of range.

Then one evening I received a visit from my cousin-brother, Charm. He'd come to me for a loan. He wanted some new bottle tips for his collection and brought me a moldy old toothbrush to offer in exchange.

Charm landed on the garden wall, toothbrush in his beak, and was waiting for me to join him there, when there was a flash and a tremendous bang. Charm was sent several feet into the air, and landed limp and dead in a flower bed.

'I've got him, I've got him!' shouted Junior *sahib*. 'I've shot that blasted crow!'

Throwing away the gun, Junior *sahib* ran out into the garden, overcome with joy. He picked up my fallen relative, and began running around the bungalow with his trophy.

The rest of the family had collected on the veranda.

'Drop that thing at once!' called the *memsahib*.

'Uncle is doing a war dance,' observed the boy.

'It's unlucky to shoot a crow,' said the Colonel.

I thought it was time to take a hand in the proceedings and let everyone know that the *right* crow—the one and only Speedy—was alive and kicking. So I swooped down the jackfruit tree, dived through Junior *sahib's* window, and emerged with one of his socks.

Triumphantly flaunting his dead crow, Junior *sahib* came dancing up the garden path, then stopped dead when he saw me perched on the window sill, a sock in my beak. His jaw fell, his eyes bulged; he looked like the owl in the banyan tree.

'You shot the wrong crow!' shouted the Colonel, and everyone roared with laughter.

Before Junior *sahib* could recover from the shock, I took off in a leisurely fashion and joined Slow on the wall.

Junior *sahib* came rushing out with the gun, but by now it was too dark to see anything, and I heard the *memsahib* telling the Colonel, 'You'd better take that gun away before he does himself a mischief.' So the Colonel took Junior indoors and gave him a brandy.

I composed a new song for Junior *sahib's* benefit, and sang it to him outside his window early next morning:

> I understand you want a crow
> To poison, shoot or smother;
> My fond salaams, but by your leave
> I'll substitute another:
> Allow me then, to introduce
> My most respected brother.

Although I was quite understanding about the whole tragic mix-up—I was, after all, the family's very own house-crow—my fellow crows were outraged at what happened to Charm, and swore vengeance on Junior *sahib*.

'*Corvus splendens!*' they shouted with great spirit, forgetting that this title had been bestowed on us by a human.

In times of war, we forget how much we owe to our enemies.

Junior *sahib* had only to step into the garden, and several crows would swoop down on him, screeching and swearing and aiming lusty blows at his head and hands. He took to coming out wearing a sola-topee, and even then they knocked it off and drove him indoors. Once he tried lighting a cigarette on the veranda steps, when Slow swooped low across the porch and snatched it from his lips.

Junior *sahib* shut himself up in his room, and smoked countless cigarettes—a sure sign that his nerves were going to pieces.

Every now and then the *memsahib* would come out and shoo us off; and because she wasn't an enemy, we obliged by retreating to the garden wall. After all, Slow and I depended on her for much of our board if not for our lodging. But Junior *sahib* had only to show his face outside the house, and all the crows in the area would be after him like avenging furies.

'It doesn't look as though they are going to forgive you,' said the *memsahib*.

'Elephants never forget, and crows never forgive,' said the Colonel.

'Would you like to borrow my catapult, Uncle?' asked the boy. 'Just for self-protection, you know.'

'Shut up,' said Junior *sahib* and went to bed.

One day he sneaked out of the back door and dashed across to the garage. A little later the family's old car, seldom used, came out of the garage with Junior *sahib* at the wheel. He'd decided that if he couldn't take a walk in safety he'd go for a drive. All the windows were up.

No sooner had the car turned into the driveway than about a dozen crows dived down on it, crowding the bonnet and flapping in front of the windscreen. Junior *sahib* couldn't see a thing. He swung the steering wheel left, right and center, and the car went off the driveway, ripped through a hedge, crushed a bed of sweet peas, and came to a stop against the trunk of a mango tree.

Junior *sahib* just sat there, afraid to open the door. The family had to come out of the house and rescue him.

'Are you all right?' asked the Colonel.

'I've bruised my knees,' said Junior *sahib*.

'Never mind our knees,' said the *memsahib*, gazing around at the ruin of her garden. 'What about my sweet peas?'

'I think your uncle is going to have a nervous breakdown,' I heard the Colonel saying.

'What's that?' asked the boy. 'Is it the same as a car having a breakdown?'

'Well—not exactly. . . .But you could call it a mind breaking up.'

Junior *sahib* had been refusing to leave his room or take his meals. The family was worried about him. I was worried, too. Believe it or not, we crows are among the very few who sincerely desire the preservation of the human species.

'He needs a change,' said the *memsahib*.

'A rest cure,' said the Colonel sarcastically. 'A rest from doing nothing.'

'Send him to Switzerland,' suggested the boy.

'We can't afford that. But we can take him up to a hill-station.'

The nearest hill-station was some fifty miles as the human drives (only ten as the crow flies). Many people went up during the summer months. It wasn't fancied much by crows.

For one thing, it was a tidy sort of place, and people lived in houses that were set fairly far apart. Opportunities for scavenging were limited. Also it was rather cold and the trees were inconvenient and uncomfortable. A friend of mine who had spent a night in a pine tree said he hadn't been able to sleep because of prickly pine needles and the wind howling through the branches.

'Let's all go up for a holiday,' said the *memsahib*. 'We can spend a week in a boarding house. All of us need a change.'

A few days later the house was locked up, and the family piled into the old car and drove off to the hills.

I had the grounds to myself.

The dog had gone too, and the gardener spent all day dozing in his hammock. There was no one around to trouble me.

'We've got the whole place to ourselves,' I told Slow.

'Yes, but what good is that? With everyone gone, there are no throw-aways, give-aways and take-aways!'

'We'll have to try the house next door.'

'And be driven off by the other crows? That's not our territory, you know. We can go across to help them, or to ask for their help, but we're not supposed to take their pickings. It just isn't cricket, old boy.'

We could have tried the bazaar or the railway station, where there is always a lot of rubbish to be found, but there is also a lot of competition in those places. The station crows are gangsters. The bazaar crows are bullies. Slow and I had grown soft. We'd have been no match for the bad boys.

'I've just realized how much we depend on humans.' I said.

'We could go back to living in the jungle,' said Slow.

'No, that would be too much like hard work. We'd be living on wild fruit most of the time. Besides, the jungle crows won't have anything to do with us now. Ever since we took up with humans, we became the outcasts of the bird world.'

'That means we're almost human.'

'You might say we have all their vices and none of their virtues.'

'Just a different set of values, old boy.'

'Like eating hens' eggs instead of crows' eggs. That's *something* in their favour. And while you're hanging around here waiting for the mangoes to fall, I'm off to locate our humans.'

Slow's beak fell open. He looked like—well, a hungry crow.

'Don't tell me you're going to follow them up to the hill-station? You don't even know where they are staying.'

'I'll soon find out,' I said, and took off for the hills.

You'd be surprised at how simple it is to be a good detective, if only you put your mind to it. Of course, if Ellery Queen had been able to fly, he wouldn't have required fifteen chapters and his father's assistance to crack a case.

Swooping low over the hill-station, it wasn't long before I spotted my humans' old car. It was parked outside a boarding house called the Climber's Rest. I hadn't seen anyone climbing, but dozing in an armchair in the garden was my favourite human.

I perched on top of a colourful umbrella and waited for Junior *sahib* to wake up. I decided it would be rather inconsiderate of me to disturb his sleep, so I waited patiently on the *brolly* , looking at him with one eye and keeping one eye on the house. He stirred uneasily, as though he'd suddenly had a bad dream; then he opened his eyes. I must have been the first thing he saw.

'Good morning,' I cawed, in a friendly tone—always ready to forgive and forget, that's Speedy!

He leapt out of the armchair and ran into the house, hollering at the top of his voice.

I supposed he hadn't been able to contain his delight at seeing me again. Humans can be funny that way. They'll hate you one day and love you the next.

Well, Junior *sahib* ran all over the boarding house, screaming: 'It's that crow, it's that crow! He's following me everywhere!'

Various people, including the family, ran outside to see what the commotion was about, and I thought it would be better to make myself scarce. So I flew to the top of a spruce tree and stayed very still and quiet.

'Crow! What crow?' said the Colonel.

'Our crow!' cried Junior *sahib*. 'The one that persecutes me. I was dreaming of it just now, and when I opened my eyes, there it was, on the garden umbrella!'

'There's nothing there now,' said the *memsahib*. 'You probably hadn't woken up completely.'

'He is having illusions again,' said the boy.

'Delusions,' corrected the Colonel.

'Now look here,' said the *memsahib*. 'You'll have to pull yourself together. You'll take leave of your senses if you don't.'

'I tell you, it's here!' sobbed Junior *sahib*. 'It's following me everywhere.'

'It's grown fond of Uncle,' said the boy. 'And it seems Uncle can't live without crows.'

Junior *sahib* looked up with a wild glint in his eye.

'That's it!' he cried. 'I can't live without them. That's the answer to my problem. I don't hate crows—I love them!'

Everyone just stood around goggling at Junior *sahib*.

'I'm feeling fine now,' he carried on. 'What a difference it makes if you can just do the opposite to what you've been doing before! I thought I hated crows. But all the time I really loved them!' And flapping his arms, and trying to caw like a crow, he went prancing about the garden.

'Now he thinks he's a crow,' said the boy. 'Is he still having delusions?'

'That's right,' said the *memsahib*. 'Delusions of grandeur.'

After that, the family decided that there was no point in staying on in the hill-station any longer. Junior *sahib* had completed his rest cure. And even if he was the only one who believed himself cured, that was all right, because after all he was the one who mattered. . . .If you're feeling fine, can there be anything wrong with you?

No sooner was everyone back in the bungalow than Junior *sahib* took to hopping barefoot on the grass early every morning, all the time scattering food about for the crows. Bread, chappatties, cooked rice, curried eggplants, the *memsahib's* homemade toffee—you name it, we got it!

Slow and I were the first to help ourselves to these dawn offerings, and soon the other crows had joined us on the lawn. We didn't mind. Junior *sahib* brought enough for everyone.

'We ought to honour him in some way,' said Slow.

'Yes, why not?' said I. 'There was someone else, hundreds of years ago, who fed the birds. They followed him wherever he went.'

'That's right. They made him a saint. But as far as I know, he didn't feed any crows. At least, you don't see any crows in the pictures—just sparrows and robins and wagtails.'

'Small fry. *Our* human is dedicated exclusively to crows. Do you realise that, Slow?'

'Sure. We ought to make him the patron saint of crows. What do you say, fellows?'

'Caw, caw, caw!' All the crows were in agreement.

'St Corvus!' said Slow, as Junior *sahib* emerged from the house, laden with good things to eat.

'Corvus, corvus, corvus!' we cried.

And what a pretty picture he made—a crow eating from his hand, another perched on his shoulder, and about a dozen of us on the grass, forming a respectful ring around him.

From persecutor to protector; from beastliness to saintliness. And sometimes it can be the other way round: you never know with humans!

A Tiger in the House

Timothy, the tiger-cub, was discovered by Grandfather on a hunting expedition in the Terai jungle near Dehra.

Grandfather was no *shikari*, but as he knew the forests of the Siwalik hills better than most people, he was persuaded to accompany the party—it consisted of several Very Important Persons from Delhi—to advise on the terrain and the direction the beaters should take once a tiger had been spotted.

The camp itself was sumptuous—seven large tents (one for each *shikari*), a dining-tent, and a number of servants' tents. The dinner was very good, as Grandfather admitted afterwards; it was not often that one saw hot-water plates, finger-glasses, and seven or eight courses, in a tent in the jungle! But that was how things were done in the days of the Viceroys. . . .There were also some fifteen elephants, four of them with howdahs for the *shikaris*, and the others especially trained for taking part in the beat.

The sportsmen never saw a tiger, nor did they shoot anything else, though they saw a number of deer, peacock, and wild boar. They were giving up all hope of finding a tiger, and were beginning to shoot at jackals, when Grandfather, strolling down the forest path at some distance from the rest of the party, discovered a little tiger about eighteen inches long, hiding among the intricate roots of a banyan tree. Grandfather picked him up, and brought him home after the camp had broken up. He had the distinction of being the only member of the party to have bagged any game, dead or alive.

At first the tiger cub, who was named Timothy by Grandmother, was brought up entirely on milk given to him in a feeding-bottle by our cook, Mahmoud. But the milk proved too rich for him, and he was put on a diet of raw mutton and cod liver oil, to be followed later by a more tempting diet of pigeons and rabbits.

Timothy was provided with two companions—Toto the monkey, who was bold enough to pull the young tiger by the tail, and then climb up the curtains if Timothy lost his temper; and a small mongrel puppy, found on the road by Grandfather.

At first Timothy appeared to be quite afraid of the puppy, and darted back with a spring if it came too near. He would make absurd dashes at it with his large forepaws, and then retreat to a ridiculously safe distance. Finally, he allowed the puppy to crawl on his back and rest there!

One of Timothy's favourite amusements was to stalk anyone who would play with him, and so, when I came to live with Grandfather, I became one of the tiger's favourites. With a crafty look in his glittering eyes, and his body crouching, he would creep closer and closer to me, suddenly making a dash for my feet, rolling over on his back and kicking with delight, and pretending to bite my ankles.

He was by this time the size of a full-grown retriever, and when I took him out for walks, people on the road would give us a wide berth. When he pulled hard on his chain, I had difficulty in keeping up with him. His favourite place in the house was the drawing-room, and he would make himself comfortable on the long sofa, reclining there with great dignity, and snarling at anybody who tried to get him off.

Timothy had clean habits, and would scrub his face with his paws exactly like a cat. He slept at night in the cook's quarters, and was always delighted at being let out by him in the morning.

'One of these days,' declared Grandmother in her prophetic manner, 'We are going to find Timothy sitting on Mahmoud's bed, and no sign of the cook except his clothes and shoes!'

Of course, it never came to that, but when Timothy was about six months old a change came over him; he grew steadily less friendly. When out for a walk with me, he would try to steal away to stalk a cat or someone's pet Pekinese. Sometimes at night we would hear frenzied cackling from the poultry house, and in the morning there would be feathers lying all over the verandah. Timothy had to be chained up more often. And finally, when he began to stalk Mahmoud about the house with what looked like villainous intent, Grandfather decided it was time to transfer him to a zoo.

The nearest zoo was at Lucknow, two hundred miles away.

Reserving a first class compartment for himself and Timothy—
no one would share a compartment with them—Grandfather
took him to Lucknow where the zoo authorities were only too
glad to receive as a gift a well-fed and fairly civilized tiger.

*

About six months later, when my grandparents were visiting
relatives in Lucknow, Grandfather took the opportunity of
calling at the zoo to see how Timothy was getting on. I was not
there to accompany him, but I heard all about it when he
returned to Dehra.

Arriving at the zoo, Grandfather made straight for the
particular cage in which Timothy had been interned. The tiger
was there, crouched in a corner, full-grown and with a
magnificent striped coat.

'Hello Timothy!' said Grandfather and, climbing the railing
with ease, he put his arm through the bars of the cage.

The tiger approached the bars, and allowed Grandfather to
put both hands around his head. Grandfather stroked the tiger's
forehead and tickled his ears, and, whenever he growled,
smacked him across the mouth, which was his old way of
keeping him quiet.

It licked Grandfather's hands and only sprang away when a
leopard in the next cage snarled at him. Grandfather 'shooed'
the leopard away, and the tiger returned to lick his hands; but
every now and then the leopard would rush at the bars, and he
would slink back to his corner.

A number of people had gathered to watch the reunion when
a keeper pushed his way through the crowd and asked
Grandfather what he was doing.

'I'm talking to Timothy,' said Grandfather. 'Weren't you here
when I gave him to the zoo six months ago?'

'I haven't been here very long,' said the surprised keeper.
'Please continue your conversation. But I have never been able
to touch him myself, he is always very bad tempered.'

'Why don't you put him somewhere else?' suggested
Grandfather. 'That leopard keeps frightening him. I'll go and see
the Superintendent about it.'

Grandfather went in search of the Superintendent of the zoo, but found that he had gone home early; and so, after wandering about the zoo for a little while, he returned to Timothy's cage to say goodbye. It was beginning to get dark.

He had been stroking and slapping Timothy for about five minutes when he found another keeper observing him with some alarm. Grandfather recognized him as the keeper who had been there when Timothy had first come to the zoo.

'*You* remember me,' said Grandfather. 'Now why don't you transfer Timothy to another cage, away from this stupid leopard?'

'But—sir—' stammered the keeper. 'It is not your tiger.'

'I know, I know,' said Grandfather testily. 'I realize he is no longer mine. But you might at least take a suggestion or two from me.'

'I remember your tiger very well,' said the keeper. 'He died two months ago.'

'Died!' exclaimed Grandfather.

'Yes, sir, of pneumonia. This tiger was trapped in the hills only last month, and he is very dangerous!'

Grandfather could think of nothing to say. The tiger was still licking his arm, with increasing relish. Grandfather took what seemed to him an age to withdraw his hand from the cage.

With his face near the tiger's he mumbled, 'Goodnight, Timothy,' and giving the keeper a scornful look, walked briskly out of the zoo.

Tiger, Tiger, Burning Bright

On the left bank of the Ganga, where it emerges from the Himalayan foothills, there is a long stretch of heavy forest. These are villages on the fringe of the forest, inhabited by bamboo-cutters and farmers, but there are few signs of commerce or pilgrimage. Hunters, however, have found the area an ideal hunting-ground during the last seventy years, and as a result the animals are not as numerous as they used to be. The trees, too, have been disappearing slowly; and, as the forest recedes, the animals lose their food and shelter and move on further into the foothills. Slowly, they are being denied the right to live.

Only the elephants can cross the river. And two years ago, when a large area of forest was cleared to make way for a refugee resettlement camp, a herd of elephants—finding their favourite food, the green shots of the bamboo, in short supply—waded across the river. They crashed through the suburbs of Hardwar, knocked down a factory wall, pulled down several tin roofs, held up a train, and left a trail of devastation in their wake until they found a new home in a new forest which was still untouched. Here, they settled down to a new life—but an unsettled, wary life. They did not know when men would appear again, with tractors, bulldozers and dynamite.

There was a time when the forest on the banks of the Ganga had provided food and shelter for some thirty or forty tigers; but men in search of trophies had shot them all, and now there remained only one old tiger in the jungle. Many hunters had tried to get him, but he was a wise and crafty old tiger, who knew the ways of men, and he had so far survived all attempts on his life.

Although the tiger had passed the prime of his life, he had lost none of his majesty. His muscles rippled beneath the golden yellow of his coat, and he walked through the long grass with

158

the confidence of one who knew that he was still a king, even though his subjects were fewer. His great head pushed through the foliage, and it was only his tail, swinging high, that showed occasionally above the sea of grass.

He was heading for water, the only water in the forest (if you don't count the river, which was several miles away), the water of a large *jheel*, which was almost a lake during the rainy season, but just a muddy marsh at this time of the year, in the late spring.

Here, at different times of the day and night, all the animals came to drink—the long-horned sambur, the delicate chital, the swamp deer, the hyaenas and jackals, the wild boar, the panthers—and the lone tiger. Since the elephants had gone, the water was usually clear except when buffaloes from the nearest village came to wallow in it, and then it was very muddy. These buffaloes, though they were not wild, were not afraid of the panther or even of the tiger. They knew the panther was afraid of their massive horns and that the tiger preferred the flesh of the deer.

One day, there were several samburs at the water's edge; but they did not stay long. The scent of the tiger came with the breeze, and there was no mistaking its strong feline odour. The deer held their heads high for a few moments, their nostrils twitching, and then scattered into the forest, disappearing behind a screen of leaf and bamboo.

When the tiger arrived, there was no other animal near the water. But the birds were still there. The egrets continued to wade in the shallows, and a kingfisher darted low over the water, dived suddenly, a flash of blue and gold, and made off with a slim silver fish, which glistened in the sun like a polished gem. A long brown snake glided in and out among the water-lilies and disappeared beneath a fallen tree which lay rotting in the shallows.

The tiger waited in the shelter of a rock, his ears pricked up for the least unfamiliar sound; for he knew that it was at that place that men sometimes sat up for him with guns; for they coveted his beauty—his stripes, and the gold of his body, his fine teeth, his whiskers, and his noble head. They would have liked to hang his skin on a wall, with his head stuffed and mounted, and pieces of glass replacing his fierce eyes; then they would have

159

boasted of their triumph over the king of the jungle.

The tiger had been hunted before, so he did not usually show himself in the open during the day. But of late he had heard no guns, and if there were hunters around, you would have heard their guns (for a man with a gun cannot resist letting it off, even if it is only at a rabbit—or at another man). And, besides, the tiger was thirsty.

He was also feeling quite hot. It was March; and the shimmering dust-haze of summer had come early. Tigers—unlike other cats—are fond of water, and on a hot day will wallow in it for hours.

He walked into the water, in amongst the water-lilies, and drank slowly. He was seldom in a hurry when he ate or drank. Other animals might bolt down their food, but they were only other animals. A tiger is a tiger; he has his dignity to preserve even though he isn't aware of it!

He raised his head and listened, one paw suspended in the air. A strange sound had come to him on the breeze, and he was wary of strange sounds. So he moved swiftly into the shelter of the tall grass that bordered the *jheel*, and climbed a hillock until he reached his favourite rock. This rock was big enough both to hide him and to give him shade. Anyone looking up from the *jheel* might think it strange that the rock had a round bump on the top. The bump was the tiger's head. He kept it very still.

The sound he heard was only the sound of a flute, rendered thin and reedy in the forest. It belonged to Ramu, a slim brown boy who rode a buffalo. Ramu played vigorously on the flute. Shyam, a slightly smaller boy, riding another buffalo, brought up the rear of the herd.

There were about eight buffaloes in the herd, and they belonged to the families of the two friends Ramu and Shyam. Their people were Gujars, a nomadic community who earned a livelihood by keeping buffaloes and selling milk and butter. The boys were about twelve years old, but they could not have told you exactly because in their village nobody thought birthdays were important. They were almost the same age as the tiger, but he was old and experienced while they were still cubs.

The tiger had often seen them at the tank, and he was not worried by their presence. He knew the village people would do him no harm as long as he left their buffaloes alone. Once when he was younger and full of bravado, he had killed a buffalo—not because he was hungry, but because he was young and wanted to try out his strength—and after that the villagers had hunted him for days, with spears, bows and an old muzzle-loader. Now he left the buffaloes alone, even though the deer in the forest were not as numerous as before.

The boys knew that a tiger lived in the jungle, for they had often heard him roar; but they did not suspect that he was so near just then.

The tiger gazed down from his rock, and the sight of eight fat black buffaloes made him give a low, throaty moan. But the boys were there, and besides—a buffalo was not easy to kill.

He decided to move on and find a cool shady place in the heart of the jungle, where he could rest during the warm afternoon and be free of the flies and mosquitoes that swarmed around the *jheel*. At night he would hunt.

With a lazy, half-humorous roar—'A-oonh!'—he got up off his haunches and sauntered off into the jungle.

Even the gentlest of the tiger's roars can be heard half a mile away, and the boys, who were barely fifty yards away, looked up immediately.

'There he goes!' said Ramu, taking the flute from his lips and pointing it towards the hillocks. He was not afraid, for he knew that this tiger was not interested in humans. 'Did you see him?'

'I saw his tail, just before he disappeared. He's a big tiger!'

'Do not call him tiger. Call him Uncle, or Maharaj.'

'Oh, why?'

'Don't you know that it's unlucky to call a tiger a tiger? My father always told me so. But if you meet a tiger, and call him Uncle, he will leave you alone.'

'I'll try and remember that,' said Shyam.

The buffaloes were now well inside the water, and some of them were lying down in the mud. Buffaloes love soft wet mud and will wallow in it for hours. The slushier the mud the better. Ramu, to avoid being dragged down into the mud with his buffalo, slipped off its back and plunged into the water. He waded to a small islet covered with reeds and water-lilies. Shyam was close behind him.

They lay down on their hard flat stomachs, on a patch of grass, and allowed the warm sun to beat down on their bare brown bodies.

Ramu was the more knowledgeable boy, because he had been to Hardwar and Dehra Dun several times with his father. Shyam had never been out of the village.

Shyam said, 'The pool is not so deep this year.'

'We have had no rain since January,' said Ramu. 'If we do not get rain soon the *jheel* may dry up altogether.'

'And then what will we do?'

'We? I don't know. There is a well in the village. But even that may dry up. My father told me that it failed once, just about the time I was born, and everyone had to walk ten miles to the river for water.'

'And what about the animals?'

'Some will stay here and die. Others will go to the river. But there are too many people near the river now—and temples, houses and factories—and the animals stay away. And the trees have been cut, so that between the jungle and the river there is no place to hide. Animals are afraid of the open—they are afraid of men with guns.'

'Even at night?'

'At night men come in jeeps, with searchlights. They kill the deer for meat, and sell the skins of tigers and panthers.'

'I didn't know a tiger's skin was worth anything.'

'It's worth more than our skins,' said Ramu knowingly. 'It will fetch six hundred rupees. Who would pay that much for one of us?'

'Our fathers would.'

'True—if they had the money.'

'If my father sold his fields, he would get more than six hundred rupees.'

'True—but if he sold his fields, none of you would have anything to eat. A man needs land as much as a tiger needs a jungle.'

'Yes,' said Shyam. 'And that reminds me—my mother asked me to take some roots home.'

'I will help you.'

They walked deeper into the *jheel* until the water was up to their waists, and began pulling up water-lilies by the roots. The flower is beautiful but the villagers value the root more. When it is cooked, it makes a delicious and strengthening dish. The plant multiples rapidly and is always in good supply. In the year when famine hit the village, it was only the root of the water-lily that saved many from starvation.

When Shyam and Ramu had finished gathering roots, they emerged from the water and passed the time in wrestling with each other, slipping about in the soft mud which soon covered them from head to toe.

To get rid of the mud, they dived into the water again and swam across to their buffaloes. Then, jumping on their backs and digging their heels into thick hides, the boys raced them across the *jheel*, shouting and hollaring so much that all the birds flew away in fright, and the monkeys set up a shrill chattering of their own in the *dhak* trees.

In March, the Flame of the Forest, or *dhak* trees, are ablaze with bright scarlet and orange flowers.

It was evening, and the twilight fading fast, when the buffalo-herd finally wended its way homeward, to be greeted outside the village by the barking of dogs, the gurgle of hookah-pipes, and the homely smell of cow-dung smoke.

*

The tiger made a kill that night—a chital. He made his approach against the wind so that the unsuspecting spotted deer did not see him until it was too late. A blow on the deer's haunches from the tiger's paw brought it down, and then the great beast fastened his fangs on the deer's throat. It was all over in a few minutes. The tiger was too quick and strong, and the deer did not struggle much.

It was a violent end for so gentle a creature. But you must not imagine that in the jungle the deer live in permanent fear of death. It is only man, with his imagination and his fear of the hereafter, who is afraid of dying. In the jungle it is different. Sudden death appears at intervals. Wild creatures do not have to think about it, and so the sudden killing of one of their number by some predator of the forest is only a fleeting incident soon forgotten by the survivors.

The tiger feasted well, growling with pleasure as he ate his way up the body, leaving the entrails. When he had his night's fill he left the carcass for the vultures and jackals. The cunning old tiger never returned to the same carcase, even if there was still plenty left to eat. In the past, when he had gone back to a kill he had often found a man sitting in a tree waiting up for him with a rifle.

His belly filled, the tiger sauntered over to the edge of the forest and looked out across the sandy wasteland and the deep, singing river, at the twinkling lights of Rishikesh on the opposite bank, and raised his head and roared his defiance at mankind.

He was a lonesome bachelor. It was five or six years since he had a mate. She had been shot by the trophy-hunters, and her two cubs had been trapped by men who do trade in wild animals. One went to a circus, where he had to learn tricks to amuse men and respond to the flick of a whip; the other, more fortunate, went first to a zoo in Delhi and was later transferred to a zoo in America.

Sometimes, when the old tiger was very lonely, he gave a great roar, which could be heard throughout the forest. The villagers thought he was roaring in anger, but the jungle knew that he was really roaring out of loneliness.

When the sound of his roar had died away, he paused, standing still, waiting for an answering roar; but it never came. It was taken up instead by the shrill scream of a barbet high up in a *sal* tree.

It was dawn now, dew-fresh and cool, and jungle-dwellers were on the move. . . .

The black beady little eyes of a jungle rat were fixed on a small brown hen who was pecking around in the undergrowth near her nest. He had a large family to feed, this rat, and he knew that in the hen's nest was a clutch of delicious fawn-coloured eggs. He waited patiently for nearly an hour before he had the satisfaction of seeing the hen leave her nest and go off in search of food.

As soon as she had gone, the rat lost no time in making his raid. Slipping quietly out of his hole, he slithered along among the leaves; but, clever as he was, he did not realize that his own movements were being watched.

A pair of grey mongooses scouted about in the dry grass. They too were hungry, and eggs usually figured large on their menu. Now, lying still on an outcrop of rock, they watched the rat sneaking along, occasionally sniffing at the air and finally vanishing behind a boulder. When he reappeared, he was struggling to roll an egg uphill towards his hole.

The rat was in difficulty, pushing the egg sometimes with his paws, sometimes with his nose. The ground was rough, and the egg wouldn't move straight. Deciding that he must have help, he scuttled off to call his spouse. Even now the mongoose did not descend on that tantalizing egg. He waited until the rat returned with his wife, and then watched as the male rat took the egg firmly between his forepaws and rolled over on to his back. The female rat then grabbed her mate's tail and began to drag him along.

Totally absorbed in their struggle with the egg, the rat did not hear the approach of the mongooses. When these two large furry visitors suddenly bobbed up from behind a stone, the rats squealed with fright, abandoned the egg, and fled for their lives.

The mongooses wasted no time in breaking open the egg and making a meal of it. But just as, a few minutes ago, the rat had not noticed their approach, so now they did not notice the village boy, carrying a small bright axe and a net bag in his hands, creeping along.

Ramu too was searching for eggs, and when he saw the mongooses busy with one, he stood still to watch them, his eyes roving in search of the nest. He was hoping the mongooses would lead him to the nest; but, when they had finished their meal and made off into the undergrowth, Ramu had to do his own searching. He failed to find the nest, and moved further into the forest. The rat's hopes were just reviving when, to his disgust, the mother hen returned.

Ramu now made his way to a *mahua* tree.

The flowers of the *mahua* can be eaten by animals as well as by men. Bears are particularly fond of them and will eat large quantities of flowers which gradually start fermenting in their stomachs with the result that the animals get quite drunk. Ramu had often seen a couple of bears stumbling home to their cave, bumping into each other or into the trunks of trees. They are short-sighted to begin with, and when drunk can hardly see at all. But their sense of smell and hearing are so good that in the end they find their way home.

Ramu decided he would gather some *mahua* flowers, and climbed up the tree, which is leafless when it blossoms. He began breaking the white flowers and throwing them to the ground. He had been on the tree for about five minutes when he heard the whining grumble of a bear, and presently a young sloth bear ambled into the clearing beneath the tree.

He was a small bear, little more than a cub, and Ramu was not frightened; but, because he thought the mother might be in the vicinity, he decided to take no change, and sat very still, waiting to see what the bear would do. He hoped it wouldn't choose the *mahua* tree for a meal.

At first the young bear put his nose to the ground and sniffed his way along until he came to a large ant-hill. Here he began huffing and puffing, blowing rapidly in and out of his nostrils, causing the dust from the ant-hill to fly in all directions. But he was a disappointed bear, because the ant-hill had been deserted long ago. And so, grumbling, he made his way across to a tall wild-plum tree, and, shinning rapidly up the smooth trunk, was soon perched on its topmost branches. It was only then that he saw Ramu.

The bear at once scrambled several feet higher up the tree, and laid himself out flat on a branch. It wasn't a very thick branch and left a large expanse of bear showing on the either side. The bear tucked his head away behind another branch, and so long as he could not see Ramu, seemed quite satisfied that he was well hidden, though he couldn't help grumbling with anxiety, for a bear, like most animals, is afraid of man.

Bears, however, are also very curious—and curiosity has often led them into trouble. Slowly, inch by inch, the young bear's black snout appeared over the edge of the branch; but immediately the eyes came into view and met Ramu's, he drew back with a jerk and the head was once more hidden. The bear did this two or three times, and Ramu, highly amused, waited until it wasn't looking, then moved some way down the tree. When the bear looked up again and saw that the boy was missing, he was so pleased with himself that he stretched right across to the next branch, to get a plum. Ramu chose this moment to burst into loud laughter. The startled bear tumbled out of the tree, dropped through the branches for a distance of some fifteen feet, and landed with a thud in a heap of dry leaves.

And then several things happened at almost the same time. The mother bear came charging into the clearing. Spotting

166

Ramu in the tree, she reared up on her hind legs, grunting fiercely. It was Ramu's turn to be startled. There are few animals more dangerous than a rampaging mother bear, and the boy knew that one blow from her clawed forepaws could rip his skull open.

But before the bear could approach the tree, there was a tremendous roar, and the old tiger bounded into the clearing. He had been asleep in the bushes not far away—he liked a good sleep after a heavy meal—and the noise in the clearing had woken him.

He was in a bad mood, and his loud 'A—oonh!' made his displeasure quite clear. The bear turned and ran from the clearing, the youngster squealing with fright.

The tiger then came into the centre of the clearing, looked up at the trembling boy, and roared again.

Ramu nearly fell out of the tree.

'Good-day to you, Uncle' he stammered, showing his teeth in a nervous grin.

Perhaps this was too much for the tiger. With a low growl, he turned his back on the *mahua* tree and padded off into the jungle, his tail twitching in disgust.

*

That night, when Ramu told his parents and his grandfather about the tiger and how it had saved him from a female bear, it started a round of tiger stories—about how some of them could be gentlemen, others rogues. Sooner or later the conversation came round to man-eaters, and Grandfather told two stories which he swore were true, although his listeners only half believed him.

The first story concerned the belief that a man-eating tiger is guided towards his next victim by the spirit of a human being previously killed and eaten by the tiger. Grandfather said that he actually knew three hunters, who sat up in a *machan* over a human kill, and that, when the tiger came, the corpse sat up and pointed with his right hand at the men in the tree. The tiger then went away. But the hunters knew he would return, and one man was brave enough to get down from the tree and tie the right arm of the corpse to its side. Later, when the tiger returned, the corpse sat up and this time pointed out the men with his left hand. The enraged tiger sprang into the tree and killed his enemies in the *machan*.

'And then there was a *bania*,' said Grandfather, beginning another story, 'who lived in a village in the jungle. He wanted to visit a neighbouring village to collect some money that was owed to him, but as the road lay through heavy forest in which lived a terrible man-eating tiger, he did not know what to do. Finally, he went to a *sadhu* who gave him two powders. By eating the first powder, he could turn into a huge tiger, capable of dealing with any other tiger in the jungle, and by eating the second he could become a *bania* again.

'Armed with his two powders, and accompanied by his pretty young wife, the *bania* set out on his journey. They had not gone far into the forest when they came upon the man-eater sitting in the middle of the road. Before swallowing the first powder, the *bania* told his wife to stay where she was, so that when he returned after killing the tiger, she could at once give him the second powder and enable him to resume his old shape.

'Well, the *bania's* plan worked, but only up to a point. He swallowed the first powder and immediately became a magnificent tiger. With a great roar, he bounded towards the man-eater, and after a brief, furious fight, killed his opponent. Then, with his jaws still dripping blood, he returned to his wife.

'The poor girl was terrified and split the second powder on the ground. The *bania* was so angry that he pounced on his wife and killed and ate her. And afterwards this terrible tiger was so enraged at not being able to become a human again that he killed and ate hundreds of people all over the country.'

'The only people he spared,' added Grandfather, with a twinkle in his eyes, 'were those who owed him money. A *bania* never gives up a loan as lost, and the tiger still hoped that one day he might become a human again and be able to collect his dues.'

Next morning, when Ramu came back from the well which was used to irrigate his father's fields, he found a crowd of curious children surrounding a jeep and three strangers with guns. Each of the strangers had a gun, and they were accompanied by two bearers and a vast amount of provisions.

They had heard that there was a tiger in the area, and they wanted to shoot it.

One of the hunters, who looked even more strange than the others, had come all the way from America to shoot a tiger, and he vowed that he would not leave the country without a tiger's skin in his baggage. One of his companions had said that he could buy a tiger's skin in Delhi, but the hunter said he preferred to get his own trophies.

These men had money to spend, and, as most of the villagers needed money badly, they were only too willing to go into the forest to construct a *machan* for the hunters. The platform, big enough to take the three men, was put up in the branches of a tall *tun*, or mahogany, tree.

It was the only night the hunters used the *machan*. At the end of March, though the days are warm, the nights are still cold. The hunters had neglected to bring blankets, and by midnight their teeth were chattering. Ramu, having tied up a buffalo calf for them at the foot of the tree, made as if to go home but instead circled the area, hanging up bits and pieces of old clothing on small trees and bushes. He thought he owed that much to the tiger. He knew the wily old king of the jungle would keep well away from the bait if he saw the bits of clothing—for where there were men's clothes, there would be men.

The vigil lasted well into the night but the tiger did not come near the *tun* tree. Perhaps he wasn't hungry; perhaps he got Ramu's message. In any case, the men in the tree soon gave themselves away.

The cold was really too much for them. A flask of rum was produced, and passed round, and it was not long before there was more purpose to finishing the rum than to finishing off a tiger. Silent at first, the men soon began talking in whispers; and to jungle creatures a human whisper is as telling as a trumpet-call.

Soon the men were quite merry, talking in loud voices. And when the first morning light crept over the forest, and Ramu and his friends came back to fetch the great hunters, they found them fast asleep in the *machan*.

The hunters looked surly and embarrassed as they trudged back to the village.

'No game left in these parts,' said the American.

'Wrong time of the year for tiger,' said the second man.

'Don't know what the country's coming to,' said the third.

And complaining about the weather, the poor quality of cartridges, the quantity of rum they had drunk, and the perversity of tigers, they drove away in disgust.

It was not until the onset of summer that an event occurred which altered the hunting habits of the old tiger and brought him into conflict with the villagers.

There had been no rain for almost two months, and the tall jungle grass had become a sea of billowy dry yellow. Some refugee settlers, living in an area where the forest had been cleared, had been careless while cooking and had started a jungle fire. Slowly it spread into the interior, from where the acrid smell and the fumes smoked the tiger out toward the edge of the jungle. As night came on, the flames grew more vivid, and the smell stronger. The tiger turned and made for the *jheel*, where he knew he would be safe provided he swam across to the little island in the centre.

Next morning he was on the island, which was untouched by the fire. But his surrounding had changed. The slopes of the hills were black with burnt grass, and most of the tall bamboo had disappeared. The deer and the wild pig, finding that their natural cover had gone, fled further east.

When the fire had died down and the smoke had cleared, the tiger prowled through the forest again but found no game. Once he came across the body of a burnt rabbit, but he could not eat it. He drank at the *jheel* and settled down in a shady spot to sleep the day away. Perhaps, by evening, some of the animals would return. If not, he too would have to look for new hunting-grounds—or a new game.

*

The tiger spent five more days looking for a suitable game to kill. By that time he was so hungry that he even resorted to rooting among the dead leaves and burnt out stumps of trees, searching for worms and beetles. This was a sad come-down for the king of the jungle. But even now he hesitated to leave the area, for he had a deep suspicion and fear of the forests further east—forests that were fast being swallowed up by human habitation.

He could have gone north, into high mountains, but they did not provide him with the long grass he needed. A panther could manage quite well up there, but not a tiger who loved the natural privacy of the heavy jungle. In the hills, he would have to hide all the time.

At break of day, the tiger came to the *jheel*. The water was now shallow and muddy, and a green scum had spread over the top. But it was still drinkable and the tiger quenched his thirst.

He lay down across his favourite rock, hoping for a deer but none came. He was about to get up and go away when he heard an animal approach.

The tiger at once leaped off his perch and flattened himself on the ground, his tawny striped skin merging with the dry grass. A heavy animal was moving through the bushes, and the tiger waited patiently.

A buffalo emerged and came to the water.

The buffalo was alone.

He was a big male, and his long curved horns lay right back across his shoulders. He moved leisurely towards the water, completely unaware of the tiger's presence.

The tiger hesitated before making his charge. It was a long time—many years—since he had killed a buffalo, and he knew the villagers would not like it. But the pangs of hunger overcame his scruples. There was no morning breeze, everything was still, and the smell of the tiger did not reach the buffalo. A monkey chattered on a nearby tree, but his warning went unheeded.

Crawling stealthily on his stomach, the tiger skirted the edge of the *jheel* and approached the buffalo from the rear. The water birds, who were used to the presence of both animals, did not raise an alarm.

Getting closer, the tiger glanced around to see if there were men, or other buffaloes, in the vicinity. Then, satisfied that he was alone, he crept forward. The buffalo was drinking, standing in shallow water at the edge of the tank, when the tiger charged from the side and bit deep into the animal's thigh.

The buffalo turned to fight, but the tendons of his right hind leg had been snapped, and he could only stagger forward a few paces. But he was a buffalo—the bravest of the domestic cattle. He was not afraid. He snorted, and lowered his horns at the tiger; but the great cat was too fast, and circling the buffalo, bit into the other hind leg.

The buffalo crashed to the ground, both hind legs crippled, and then the tiger dashed in, using both tooth and claw, biting deep into the buffalo's throat until the blood gushed out from the jugular vein.

The buffalo gave one long, last bellow before dying.

The tiger, having rested, now began to gorge himself, but, even though he had been starving for days, he could not finish the huge carcase. At least one good meal still remained, when, satisfied and feeling his strength returning, he quenched his thirst at the *jheel*. Then he dragged the remains of the buffalo into the bushes to hide it from the vultures, and went off to find a place to sleep.

He would return to the kill when he was hungry.

The villagers were upset when they discovered that a buffalo was missing; and next day, when Ramu and Shyam came running home to say that they found the carcase near the *jheel*, half eaten by a tiger, the men were disturbed and angry. They felt that the tiger had tricked and deceived them. And they knew that once he got a taste for domestic cattle, he would make a habit of slaughtering them.

Kundan Singh, Shyam's father and the owner of the dead buffalo, said he would go after the tiger himself.

'It is all very well to talk about what you will do to the tiger,' said his wife, 'but you should never have let the buffalo go off on its own.'

'He had been out on his own before,' said Kundan. 'This is the first time the tiger has attacked one of our beasts. A devil must have entered the Maharaj.'

'He must have been very hungry,' said Shyam.

'Well, we are hungry too,' said Kundan Singh.

'Our best buffalo—the only male in our herd.'

'The tiger will kill again,' said Ramu's father.

'If we let him,' said Kundan.

'Should we send for the *shikaris*?'

'No. They were not clever. The tiger will escape them easily. Besides, there is no time. The tiger will return for another meal tonight. We must finish him off ourselves!'

'But how?'

Kundan Singh smiled secretively, played with the ends of his moustache for a few moments, and then, with great pride, produced from under his cot a double-barrelled gun of ancient vintage.

'My father bought it from an Englishman,' he said.

'How long ago was that?'

'At the time I was born.'

'And have you ever used it?' asked Ramu's father, who was not sure that the gun would work.

'Well, some years back, I let it off at some bandits. You remember the time when those dacoits raided our village? They chose the wrong village, and were severely beaten for their pains. As they left, I fired my gun off at them. They didn't stop running until they crossed the Ganga!'

'Yes, but did you hit anyone?'

'I would have, if someone's goat hadn't got in the way at the last moment. But we had roast mutton that night! Don't worry, brother, I know how the thing fires.'

Accompanied by Ramu's father and some others, Kundan set out for the *jheel*, where, without shifting the buffalo's carcase— for they knew that the tiger would not come near them if he suspected a trap—they made another *machan* in the branches of a tall tree some thirty feet from the kill.

Later that evening—at the hour of cow-dust—Kundan Singh and Ramu's father settled down for the night on their crude platform in the tree.

Several hours passed, and nothing but a jackal was seen by the watchers. And then, just as the moon came up over the distant hills, Kundan and his companion were startled by a low 'A-ooonh', followed by a suppressed, rumbling growl.

Kundan grasped his old gun, whilst his friend drew closer to him for comfort. There was complete silence for a minute or two—time that was an agony of suspense for the watchers— and then the sound of stealthy footfalls on dead leaves under the trees.

A moment later the tiger walked out into the moonlight and stood over his kill.

At first Kundan could do nothing. He was completely overawed by the size of this magnificent tiger. Ramu's father had to nudge him, and then Kundan quickly put the gun to his shoulder, aimed at the tiger's head, and pressed the trigger.

The gun went off with a flash and two loud bangs, as Kundan fired both barrels. Then there was a tremendous roar. One of the bullets had grazed the tiger's head.

The enraged animal rushed at the tree and tried to leap up into the branches. Fortunately the *machan* had been built at a safe height, and the tiger was unable to reach it. It roared again and then bounded off into the forest.

*

'What a tiger!' exclaimed Kundan, half in fear and half in admiration. 'I feel as though my liver has turned to water.'

'You missed him completely,' said Ramu's father, 'Your gun makes big noise; an arrow would have done more damage.'

'I did not miss him,' said Kundan, feeling offended, 'You heard him roar, didn't you? Would he have been so angry if he had not been hit? If I have wounded him badly, he will die.'

'And if you have wounded him slightly, he may turn into a man-eater, and then where will we be?'

'I don't think he will come back,' said Kundan. 'He will leave these forests.'

They waited until the sun was up before coming down from the tree. They found a few drops of blood on the dry grass but no trail led into the forest, and Ramu's father was convinced that the wound was only a slight one.

The bullet, missing the fatal spot behind the ear, had only grazed the back of the skull and cut a deep groove at its base. It took a few days to heal, and during this time the tiger lay low and did not go near the *jheel* except when it was very dark and he was very thirsty.

The villagers thought the tiger had gone away, and Ramu and Shyam—accompanied by some other youths, and always carrying axes and *lathis*—began bringing buffaloes to the tank again during the day; but they were careful not to let any of them stray far from the herd, and they returned home while it was still daylight.

It was some days since the jungle had been ravaged by the fire, and in the tropics the damage is repaired quickly. In spite of it being the dry season, new life was creeping into the forest.

While the buffaloes wallowed in the muddy water, and the

boys wrestled on their grassy islet, a big tawny eagle soared high above them, looking for a meal—a sure sign that some of the animals were beginning to return to the forest. It was not long before his keen eyes detected a movement in the glade below.

What the eagle with its powerful eyesight saw was a baby hare, a small fluffy thing, its long pink-tinted ears laid flat along its sides. Had it not been creeping along between two large stones, it would have escaped notice. The eagle waited to see if the mother was about, and as he waited he realized that he was not the only one who coveted this juicy morsel. From the bushes there had appeared a sinuous yellow creature, pressed low to the ground and moving rapidly towards the hare. It was a yellow jungle cat, hardly noticeable in the scorched grass. With great stealth the jungle cat began to stalk the baby hare.

He pounced. The hare's squeal was cut short by the cat's cruel claws; but it had been heard by the mother hare, who now bounded into the glade and without the slightest hesitation went for the surprised cat.

There was nothing haphazard about the mother hare's attack. She flashed around behind the cat and jumped clean over it. As she landed, she kicked back, sending a stinging jet of dust shooting into the cat's face. She did this again and again.

The bewildered cat, crouching and snarling, picked up the kill and tried to run away with it. But the hare would not permit this. She continued her leaping and buffeting, till eventually the cat, out of sheer frustration, dropped the kill and attacked the mother.

The cat sprung at the hare a score of times, lashing out with its claws; but the mother hare was both clever and agile enough to keep just out of reach of those terrible claws, and drew the cat further and further away from her baby—for she did not as yet know that it was dead.

The tawny eagle saw his chance. Swift and true, he swooped. For a brief moment, as his wings overspread the furry little hare and his talons sank deep into it, he caught a glimpse of the cat racing towards him and the mother hare fleeing into the bushes. And then with a shrill 'kee-ee-ee' of triumph, he rose and whirled away with his dinner.

The boys had heard his shrill cry and looked up just in time to see eagle flying over the *jheel* with the small little hare held firmly in its talons.

'Poor hare,' said Shyam. 'Its life was short.'

'That's the law of the jungle,' said Ramu. 'The eagle has a family too, and must feed it.'

'I wonder if we any better than animals,' said Shyam.

'Perhaps we are a little better, in some ways,' said Ramu. 'Grandfather always says, "To be able to laugh and to be merciful are the only things that make man better than the beast."'

The next day, while the boys were taking the herd home, one of the buffaloes lagged behind. Ramu did not realize that the animal was missing until he heard an agonized bellow behind him. He glanced over his shoulder just in time to see the big striped tiger dragging the buffalo into a clump of young bamboo. At the same time the herd became aware of the danger, and the buffaloes snorted with fear as they hurried along the forest path. To urge them forward, and to warn his friends, Ramu cupped his hands to his mouth and gave vent to a yodelling call.

The buffaloes bellowed, the boys shouted, and the birds flew shrieking from the trees. It was almost a stampede by the time the herd emerged from the forest. The villagers heard the thunder of hoops, and saw the herd coming home amidst clouds of dust and confusion, and knew that something was wrong.

'The tiger!' shouted Ramu. 'He is here! He has killed one of the buffaloes.'

'He is afraid of us no longer,' said Shyam.

'Did you see where he went?' asked Kundan Singh, hurrying up to them.

'I remember the place,' said Ramu. 'He dragged the buffalo in amongst the bamboo.'

'The there is no time to lose,' said his father. 'Kundan, you take your gun and two men, and wait near the suspension bridge, where the Garur stream joins the Ganga. The jungle is narrow there. We will beat the jungle from our side, and drive the tiger towards you. He will not escape us, unless he swims the river!'

'Good!' said Kundan, running into his house for his gun, with Shyam close at his heels. 'Was it one of our buffaloes again?' he asked.

'It was Ramu's buffalo this time,' said Shyam. 'A good milk buffalo.'

'Then Ramu's father will beat the jungle thoroughly. You boys had better come with me. It will not be safe for you to accompany the beaters.'

*

Kundan Singh, carrying his gun and accompanied by Ramu, Shyam and two men, headed for the river junction, while Ramu's father collected about twenty men from the village and, guided by one of the boys who had been with Ramu, made for the spot where the tiger had killed the buffalo.

The tiger was still eating when he heard the men coming. He had not expected to be disturbed so soon. With an angry 'whoof!' he bounded into a bamboo thicket and watched the men through a screen of leaves and tall grass.

The men did not seem to take much notice of the dead buffalo, but gathered round their leader and held a consultation. Most of them carried hand-drums slung from their shoulder. They also carried sticks, spears and axes.

After a hurried conversation, they entered the denser part of the jungle, beating their drums with the palms of their hands. Some of the men banged empty kerosene tins. These made even more noise than the drums.

The tiger did not like the noise and retreated deeper into the jungle. But he was surprised to find that men, instead of going away, came after him into the jungle, banging away on their drums and tins, and shouting at the top of their voices. They had separated now, and advanced single or in pairs, but nowhere were they more than fifteen yards apart. The tiger could easily have broken through this slowly advancing semi-circle of men—one swift blow from his paw would have felled the strongest of them—but his main aim was to get away from the noise. He hated and feared noise made by men.

He was not a man-eater and he would not attack a man unless he was very angry or frightened or very desperate; and he was none of these things as yet. He had eaten well, and he would have liked to rest in peace—but there would be no rest for any animal until the men ceased their tremendous clatter and din.

For an hour Ramu's father and others beat the jungle, calling, drumming and trampling the undergrowth. The tiger had no rest. Whenever he was able to put some distance between himself and the men, he would sink down in some shady spot to rest; but, within five or ten minutes, the trampling and drumming would sound nearer, and the tiger, with an angry snarl, would get up and pad north, pad silently north along the narrowing strip of jungle, towards the junction of the Garur stream and the Ganga. Ten years back, he would have had the jungle on his right in which to hide; but the trees had been felled long ago, to make way for humans and houses, and now he could only move to the left, towards the river.

It was about noon when the tiger finally appeared in the open. He longed for the darkness and security of the night, for the sun was his enemy. Kundan and the boys had a clear view of him as he stalked slowly along, now in the open with the sun glinting on his glossy side, now in the shade or passing through the shorter reeds. He was still out of range of Kundan's gun, but there was no fear of his getting out of the beat, as the 'stops' were all picked men from the village. He disappeared among some bushes but soon reappeared to retrace his steps, the beaters having done their work well. He was now only one hundred and fifty yards from the rocks where Kundan Singh waited, and he looked very big.

The beat had closed in, and the exit along the bank down stream was completely blocked, so the tiger turned into a belt of reeds, and Kundan Singh expected that the head would soon peer out of the cover a few yards away. The beaters were now making a great noise, shouting and beating their drums, but nothing moved; and Ramu, watching from a distance, wondered, 'Has he slipped through the beaters?' And he half hoped so.

Tins clashed, drums beat, and some of the men poked into the reeds with their spears or long bamboos. Perhaps one these thrusts found a mark, because at last the tiger was roused, and with an angry desperate snarl he charged out of the reeds, splashing his way through an inlet of mud and water.

Kundan Singh fired, and his bullet struck the tiger on the thigh.

The mighty animal stumbled; but he was up in a minute, and rushing through a gap in the narrowing line of beaters, he made straight for the only way across the river—the suspension bridge that passed over the Ganga here, providing a route into the high hills beyond.

'We'll get him now,' said Kundan, priming his gun again. 'He's right in the open!'

The suspension bridge swayed and trembled as the wounded tiger lurched across it. Kundan fired, and this time the bullet grazed the tiger's shoulder. The animal bounded forward, lost his footing on the unfamiliar, slippery planks of the swaying bridge, and went over the side, falling headlong into the strong, swirling waters of the river.

He rose to the surface once, but the current took him under and away, and only a thin streak of blood remained on the river's surface.

Kundan and others hurried down stream to see if the dead tiger had been washed up on the river's banks; but though they searched the riverside several miles, they did not find the king of the forest.

*

He had not provided anyone with a trophy. His skin would not be spread on a couch, nor would his head be hung up on a wall. No claw of his would be hung up on a wall. No claw of his would be hung as a charm around the neck of a child. No villager would use his fat as a cure for rheumatism.

At first the villagers were glad because they felt their buffaloes were safe. Then the men began to feel that something had gone out of their lives, out of the life of the forest; they began to feel that the forest was no longer a forest. It had been shrinking year by year, but, as long as the tiger had been there and the villagers had heard it roar at night, they had known that they were still secure from the intruders and newcomers who came to fell the trees and eat up the land and let the flood waters into the village. But, now that the tiger had gone, it was as though a protector had gone, leaving the forest open and vulnerable, easily destroyable. And, once the forest was destroyed, they too would be in danger....

There was another thing that had gone with the tiger, another thing that had been lost, a thing that was being lost everywhere—something called 'nobility'.

Ramu remembered something that his grandfather had once said, 'The tiger is the very soul of India, and when the last tiger has gone, so will the soul of the country.'

The boys lay flat on their stomachs on their little mud island and watched the monsoon clouds, gathering overhead.

'The king of our forest is dead,' said Shyam. 'There are no more tigers.'

'There must be tigers,' said Ramu. 'How can there be an India without tigers?'

The river had carried the tiger many miles away from its home, from the forest it had always known, and brought it ashore on a strip of warm yellow sand, where it lay in the sun, quite still, but breathing.

Vultures gathered and waited at a distance, some of them perching on the branches of nearby trees.

But the tiger was more drowned than hurt, and as the river water oozed out of his mouth, and the warm sun made new life throb through his body, he stirred and stretched, and his glazed eyes came into focus. Raising his head, he saw trees and tall grass.

Slowly he heaved himself off the ground and moved at a crouch to where the grass waved in the afternoon breeze. Would he be harried again, and shot at? There was no smell of Man. The tiger moved forward with greater confidence.

There was, however, another smell in the air—a smell that reached back to the time when he was young and fresh and full of vigour—a smell that he had almost forgotten but could never quite forget—the smell of a tigress!

He raised his head high, and new life surged through his tired limbs. He gave a full-throated roar and moved purposefully through the tall grass. And the roar came back to him, calling him, calling him forward—a roar that meant there would be more tigers in the land!

PENGUIN ONLINE